THE CAMPUS DETECTIVE

The Sociopath

Dave Larson

Order this book online at www.trafford.com
or email orders@trafford.com

Most Trafford titles are also available at major online book retailers.

Printed in the United States of America.

ISBN: 978-1-4269-4980-7 (sc)
ISBN: 978-1-4269-4981-4 (e)

Trafford rev. 12/28/2010

 www.trafford.com

North America & international
toll-free: 1 888 232 4444 (USA & Canada)
phone: 250 383 6864 ♦ fax: 812 355 4082

To my family:

and

The University of Washington Police Department

DWL

Also by Dave Larson:

The Bear Hunters 2007
It's About Time 2010

Contents

Preface

The characters in this book are fictitious and the incidences portrayed came from my imagination, except in some cases where they were inspired by real events.

While a student at the University of Washington, I took a part-time job with the Campus Police Department. As an unarmed security guard, I would walk a beat during the middle of the night, and I never knew what to expect. If I sensed something dangerous, I would find a phone and call for a regular armed police officer.

My duties also included helping the regular officers providing security for VIP visitors. I once waved Harry S. Truman's visiting entourage on to the campus; I helped to protect President John F. Kennedy who came to deliver a commencement address; I watched over England's Prince Phillip during his visit to the Fisheries Department; and I helped to protect the American Nazi Party leader, George Lincoln Rockwell from an irate audience as he gave a speech on campus.

Most days were not as exciting or interesting as depicted in this book. I just checked out buildings, turned off lights and locked doors. But, the occasional surprises I encountered and the many stories I heard, gave me an education that was as rich as my academic studies.

Dave Larson
11/04/2010

Chapter 1
The Case for Superman

Professor Anders of the math department climbed the stairs of the stage, and stepped up to the lectern to address his audience assembled at the University of Washington Faculty Club. He was a jovial man in his late fifties, with a shock of reddish wavy hair. He was a little overweight, probably from too many buffet dinners. He was dressed in brown slacks and a tweed sport coat. He had never been seen to wear a tie, and his tan shirt was unbuttoned at the collar. He seemed a relaxed and pleasant fellow.

"Good evening," he said into the microphone. "It's nice to see you all again at the Tuesday Evening Faculty Lectures. I hope everyone has gotten enough to eat. It looks like there's plenty left for seconds, or even thirds," he said as he gestured with his hand toward the buffet table.

He paused for a minute to let people settle in.

"If this is your first time to a lecture of these series, let me explain what this is about. For three years now, we have been having this informal forum here in the Faculty Club. We share information about new or interesting discoveries in our fields. We meet at 7:00 on the third Tuesday evening of every month that school is in session. We rotate by department, and this month it's the Sociology Department's turn.

He paused to give a few people time to take another helping of roast beef or salad, refresh their drinks, and then return to their seats at the round tables that were spread throughout the dining room. Finally, everyone was seated and those who had their backs to the podium turned their chairs around so they could see.

Professor Anders was satisfied the audience was now attentive, and he began his opening remarks.

"Tonight our speaker is Professor Michael Hunter who will tell us about new research he is doing on profiling and type classifying of criminals. Dr. Hunter is a well-known criminologist and has written several books and articles on the subject, and he has been a consultant to law enforcement agencies across the country. He has even been an interim warden at the McNeil Island Penitentiary. I'm sure he'll have a most interesting lecture. Please welcome Dr. Michael Hunter.

Hunter, a large man, who was wearing grey slacks and a sport coat, stood up from a chair at one of the front tables. He turned and smiled at the audience as they applauded him. He climbed the stage stairs after allowing Anders to come down and find his place at a table.

Hunter walked briskly to the podium and stood before his colleagues. He wore wire rimmed glasses and his dark hair was beginning to show patches of grey, giving his age to be in the mid-fifties. Because of his size and demeanor, he could have easily been mistaken for the football coach.

There was, however, one unusual thing about him. He kept his left hand jammed down into the pocket of his coat, but enough could be seen revealing a black leather glove.

"Good evening," he began with a warm friendly smile.

"I have a few preliminary remarks I'd like to make before I give my talk. I'm sure many of you here tonight have taken at least a survey course in Sociology when you were undergraduates. However, some of you, especially those who are in the 'hard sciences' and engineering, have been known to have doubts as to whether the Social Sciences qualifies as a 'real science.'

"It's true that Sociology covers a broad spectrum of collective human behavior phenomena, which may include studying the behavior of people during a disaster, or soccer fans rioting, or like my good friend and fellow Sociologist, Dr. Cal Schmid, who specializes in demography and socio-statistics.

"I believe some areas of Sociology can be as scientific as Chemistry or Physics or any other discipline using the 'scientific method' of research. In the past, social scientists would write subjective reports that would cast suspicion on their work, such as personality type studies made by 'mapping' bumps on a person's scull, or by classifying behavior predictions based on body physiques.

"But, in these days, we teach our students the importance of using the scientific method by statistical measurements and observations. Any research not backed by these tools is generally not accepted for publication. Now, with that out of the way, I'm ready to talk about my work on the behaviors of a certain criminal type known as the Sociopath."

Hunter paused a few seconds to change gears.

"My area of interest is criminology, which includes studies and research in Police Sciences, Forensics, and Prison Management to name a few. However, the most interesting is the relatively new field of profiling criminal types. I say '*new*,' but it really isn't. People have been profiling criminals for many years. We all do. A suspected perpetrator of a heinous crime, who is scruffy looking and perhaps black, is more likely to be condemned in the minds of citizens than a suspect who is white and college educated. This form of profiling has sent many innocent people to prison, and unfortunately, even to the gallows.

"What *is* new in profiling is the use of genetics. We've all become aware of the use of DNA in solving certain crimes. When DNA evidence is found at the scene of a crime and matches the DNA of a suspect, the case is solved. But, what if we find a gene that is mostly common in individuals who are incarcerated for violent crimes. This is what I'm actively researching now.

The professor paused a moment to take a drink of water from a glass on the podium. He briefly looked down at his notes, and then again fixed his gaze on his audience and continued.

"I started my research while I was the interim warden at McNeil Island, and I have several graduate students that are helping me process the data that I've collected. I decided to select inmates who were deemed antisocial or sociopathic as subjects from which to collect biological samples. The reason I chose sociopaths is because they have common traits that are easy to identify. A sociopath is the kind of guy everyone steers away from. He is brutal, vicious and is by *far* the most dangerous animal in the world. He is unpredictable and has no feeling of empathy, or kindness. He has a schizoid personality with no emotions. These guys are constantly working out in the prison gym by lifting weights and other body building exercises. They want to be strong enough to rip a person to pieces like Hannibal Lecter in the movie, 'Silence of the Lambs.'"

Dr. Hunter again paused for a few seconds and was pleased to see everyone sitting upright and paying attention. Then he continued.

"You may have heard the term, '*Psychopath*.' Everyone, at one time or another, has been in contact with a Psychopath. They are all around you.

He might be a salesman trying to sell you a car, or a teacher, or your next door neighbor. He might even be the successful CEO of a large company. Basically, he is the self-centered individual who doesn't worry about hurting people's feelings. I'm sure you must know someone like that.

"It's when the Psychopath has crossed the line and commits a crime of violence that he has earned the title of '*Sociopath*.'

"One way of looking at it is, all Sociopaths are Psychopaths, but not all Psychopaths are Sociopaths. Then, I realized there is a sub species of the sociopath that is even more violent and more intelligent than the average. With help from Professor William Barnes of the Human Physiology Department, we have found identifiable characteristics for this animal and we have given him a name. We call him, '*Superman!*'"

Professor Hunter paused again for a drink and the audience broke into a buzz of conversation about his claim. He quickly brought them back to order with his broad smile, and then continued.

"This is not to be confused in any way with the good Superman who saves Lois Lane and at times the world."

Laughter filled the room, relieving the tensions from this stunning proclamation.

"I am sure you are all eager to hear more, so I'll let Dr. Barnes explain."

Professor Hunter stepped back from the podium as a thin, young, bookish looking man in a brown suit arose from the same table as Hunter had been sitting. He was about thirty years of age, with horn rimmed glasses, and appeared agile and energetic. He acknowledged the complimentary applause with a smile, took a moment to collect his thoughts, and then he began.

"Thank you for inviting me to your monthly gathering. First of all, I want you to know it was Dr. Hunter who suggested and initiated the idea there was, perhaps, something physically unusual about some of the men who were not only incarcerated here in Washington State, but in every prison in the world. "Dr. Hunter called me one day several months ago and asked if I'd be interested in participating in a research study to find the genetic marker identifying a person as being a 'Superman.' Now, my first reactions were probably the same as yours. I thought he was joking, but then, why would he joke?

"We knew, of course, all women have two X chromosomes genetically, and men have one X and one Y chromosome. But, the question he put to me was this. Is it possible some that men, through a defect, could end up with one X and two Y chromosomes?

"Now, I understood what he was talking about. I had heard of such a genetic anomaly, but I wasn't aware of any studies about it. He then asked how such men would behave. My response was, without an observation study, I had no idea.

"He then showed me documented observations and genetic samples of over a hundred men.

"That's how our alliance started. He provided the samples and the observation documentation, and I discovered over 10% of the samples were from men with an extra Y chromosome. *Supermen*!

"Most of the men who tested positive were taken from a population he observed to have sociopathic traits. However, we also found some positives in other inmates, where the crimes they committed were especially violent."

Hunter now stepped back to the microphone.

"Thank you, Bill. I know it's getting late, but I wanted to save some time for questions."

"Michael," called out a voice from the audience, "you once mentioned you had a serial killer in one of your classes."

"Yes. That's right."

"What kind of grade did you give him?"

The question caused some laughter.

"I gave him an 'A'. But, he deserved an 'A'. He was an excellent student. But, something happened to him. It was like a switch was suddenly turned on. He became a killer. I could never imagine him to become the second most prolific serial killer in the U.S. He paid the price in the electric chair. No one knows if he fit the 'Superman' profile or not. He specifically targeted beautiful young women, and his crimes were extremely violent. Based on that, I would guess he probably would have tested positive. He certainly was a sociopath because of his lack of empathy. Anyone of us here today could be the target of such a vile animal and never make it home tonight. There is a thought he may have been suffering from multiple personalities, one of which was a sociopath."

A comment came from the audience.

"Dr. Hunter, do you say all Sociopaths are not necessarily 'Supermen?'"

"They are not. I think the 'Supermen' to be a subgroup of those considered to be Sociopaths. In the study made by Dr. Barnes, not all Sociopaths were found to have the 'super' chromosome. Also, there were a few individuals who were not Sociopaths who had the extra chromosome and have never committed a crime. So, perhaps, there is a blending of personalities. I wanted to find the pure factors leading to the identification of the '*Superman Syndrome*'. I am trying to type the classification rather than the individual."

"Dr. Hunter, didn't you take over the job of warden at the McNeil Island penitentiary for a time?"

"Yes, for one year. The warden at that time was Will Holdem, and for some reason, he disappeared. To this day, no one knows what happened to him. Some thought he might have been murdered by a previous inmate, but there was never any evidence found to support that idea. His family said he seemed to be under a lot of stress, and they are hoping he'll be found some day, perhaps suffering from amnesia."

Hands went up again.

"Let's see, yes! Dr. Reasoner."

"Michael, how were you chosen to fill in for Warden Holdem?"

"Yes, well, with my research work and teaching in criminology, I suppose. I've never had any hands-on experience in the prison system. I'd written to Warden Holdem and asked if I could spend some time at the prison to perform studies on criminal types. His response back to me was negative. He felt this would be patronizing the inmates, and Holdem's management method was to show no interest in them at all. After Holdem disappeared, Governor Headmann asked me if I would fill in for the remaining year on the warden's contract. I jumped at the chance, and a colleague was willing to take over my classes."

"Wasn't there a riot at the prison while you were there?" asked Reasoner.

"Yes there was," said Hunter. "I hope no one is blaming *me* for that," he quipped.

The audience responded with laughter.

"Weren't you taken hostage?" asked Dr. Rainey of the Psychology Department.

"No, not exactly. Actually, I presented myself to the rioting prisoners to hear their demands. As it turned out, the prisoners for the most part were cooperative when they realized I was not like my predecessor. I promised there would be no punishment if they would return to their cells and allow me to deal with the instigators."

"And did that happen?" asked Rainey.

"Yes, except for one individual. He was the one responsible for the melee. The other inmates were afraid of him. He was the most *hated* and *feared* person that walked the Earth. Although I was never able to test him, there is little doubt he was a Sociopath with the extra chromosome. The crimes he committed were the most heinous. He managed to escape during the uproar, and was gone before I even met with the prisoners. He is still at large and must be found before he goes on a wild murdering spree."

Dr. Anders asked, "Michael, how were you able to gather the information for your book, 'The Sociopath?'"

"Through trust. I gave them small privileges, and they allowed me to collect data and samples."

"Well, folks," said Dr. Anders. "We have time for one more question."

Bernie Bunsen of the Chemistry Department raised his hand.

"Yes," said Hunter.

"What happened to your hand?"

Hunter was taken aback.

"*What?*" he asked.

"What's wrong with your left hand? Why do you wear a glove on it?"

"What does this have to do with what I've been talking about?" Hunter asked sharply.

Bunsen was getting some cross looks from others in the audience.

"Does it have something to do with the riot?"

Professor Hunter took a moment to compose himself, and then he looked directly at Bunsen.

"I'm upset you'd ask about that," said Hunter. "The answer to your question is, *yes*, but that is all I'll say about it."

Then Professor Anders rose from his chair to close the session.

"Well, that's it for tonight, folks. Let's give our speakers a hand."

The attendees politely applauded Drs. Hunter and Barnes as they stepped down from the stage, then many made their way back to the bar for a final drink. A young man, George Wesson, made his way through the crowd to greet Dr. Hunter.

"That was great, Michael. Thank you for inviting me."

"It's my pleasure, George."

Chapter 2
A Dead Body On Campus

The University of Washington Seattle campus is a mixture of more than 63,000 faculty, staff and students, and 220 buildings spread over 643 acres, comparable to a medium sized city. To keep the peace and manage traffic is the responsibility of the campus police force. From the early morning until the last evening class is taught, the police department is busy with traffic enforcement, accidents, sporting event crowds and disturbances of all kinds.

But, it's the hours between ten PM and seven AM when the campus streets become like any other city street. Those are the hours when some of the most bizarre things happen. It's also the hours when only a few security guards and police officers are on duty. Three officers are on car patrol, two are on foot patrol, one desk officer takes phone calls and operates the radio base station, and one officer is the graveyard shift commander.

Early one Fall Friday morning, about five-thirty, the desk officer answered the phone.

"University Police, Officer Hanson speaking."

"Um, I just found a dead body," said a stressed young male's voice.

"What is your name, please?"

"Daryl Johnson."

"Daryl Johnson? Aren't you the football team's quarterback?"

"Um, yeah," said a nervous voice.

"Are you near the body now?"

"Yeah, I'm using a cell phone."

"OK. Are you on the campus?"

"Yeah, I'm on the perimeter road, just north of the big smoke stack."

"OK. Hang on a minute."

Officer Hanson keyed the radio microphone.

"Car 3?" he called.

"Car 3, go ahead," came the response.

"Car 3, meet the man on the perimeter road, north of the physical plant."

"10-4," the patrol officer responded.

Then back to the phone.

"Daryl, you should soon see some headlights from one of our patrol cars coming from the north.

"OK."

"Show him what you've found."

"I think I see him coming now."

"Car 3, 10-7 on perimeter road," announced the patrol car driver that he was on the scene.

"10-4," acknowledged Hanson.

Officer John Hanson leaned back in his chair. There wasn't much else to do but wait for car 3, Officer Phil Owens, to call in to tell him what he's got. The shift commander, Sergeant Bob Jones, came out of his office. He overheard the radio exchanges and came out to hear Phil's report.

"Radio, this is car 3."

"Go ahead."

"We have a DB (dead body). Looks like a young female."

"10-4. Stand by."

"I'll take car 4 up there," said Sgt. Jones. "Call the Coroner and Lt. Wesson."

"OK, Sarge."

Officer Hanson's first call was to the county coroner to report the body, and then he called Lieutenant George Wesson at his home.

When Lt. Wesson awoke at five forty-five to the ringing of his phone, he knew something was going on at the campus.

"Hello, Wesson," he answered, trying to emerge from the fog of sleep.

"Morning, George. We've found a body on campus."

"Oh, yeah? Where?"

"It's alongside of the perimeter road, north of the physical plant."

"Is anyone protecting the scene?"

"Phil Owens is at the scene, and Sgt. Jones is on his way there."

"Good. Tell them not to let anyone touch anything. I'll be at the office within thirty minutes."

Wesson hung up the phone, hurriedly got dressed, kissed his wife, and went out the door. Heading south on the freeway from his home in the town of Edmonds, he didn't encounter much traffic at this early hour.

He'd been with the Campus Police Force, part-time, for seven years, while he was a student. After finishing his master's degree in Criminology, he was hired full-time as a patrol officer, and then advanced to the rank of lieutenant and became a detective.

But, all had not gone well for him as a student. He suffered from neurotic anxiety that threatened his ability to perform while under stress. This became evident as he faced midterm and final examinations. Even though he knew the material well, he would often break into a sweat, his heart would pound and his mind would go blank. However, two things happened that saved his academic career and possibly his very life.

George Wesson decided to go to the campus health clinic for help. He ended up seeing a psychologist, Dr. Annie Alanson, who treated him with psychotherapy. About this same time, Professor Michael Hunter noticed him and saw potential in him. He became Wesson's mentor and friend. These two people had a profound effect on his life and caused his confidence and abilities to soar. But, the anxiety problem was still there, just below the surface, and from time to time would raise its head.

Now, at the age of thirty-one, he had infused vigor into the Investigations Department. He was beginning to put on a little weight, but he was in excellent physical condition.

The department had been a one man office for years, and when Stan Nelson became sixty-five he retired. The reigns were then handed to Wesson. The first thing he did was to hit the chief up for an additional man.

"What do you need another man for?" asked the chief. "We've been getting by with one man for years."

"*Getting by*, are the right words, Chief. How did Stan handle most of his investigations?"

"Sometimes he'd get SPD (Seattle Police Department) involved."

"And what's been SPD's attitude about helping us lately?"

Chief Meyers was getting annoyed being grilled by this young upstart, Wesson.

"Look, I see your point," said the chief. "I'll put in a request for one man at the next budget meeting. Do you have anyone in mind?"

"Yes, I want Danny Smith."

"Smith? He's pretty young," said the chief.

"Sure. But, he's got a degree."

The chief made a note to himself, and then looked at Wesson, "Anything else?"

"Yeah, I want Smith to start working with me right away."

Then the chief blew up.

"*Wesson!*" he shouted. "Get outa my office!"

Wesson smiled to himself as he remembered the incident. Danny Smith had been working with him ever since, and they got along well. He and Danny made a point of solving their own cases and not calling in SPD. The two men were successful in recovering most stolen property and arresting the thieves.

He arrived at the police office, parked his car in the lot, and went into the building. Officer Hanson was seated at a desk, with a radio mike and telephone.

"Hello John. Busy night?"

"Not until about an hour ago."

"Is the coroner here yet?

"No. They're scheduled to be here around 8 o'clock"

"Are they so busy they have to schedule their appointments now?"

"I guess it's a sign of the times."

Wesson shook his head and then went to his office. He unlocked the door, entered the room and pulled out a black case from his coat closet and a 9 MM Glock service automatic which he strapped to his left shoulder. He picked up the bag, relocked the door and went back to Hanson's desk.

"John, give me the keys to car 5."

Hanson reached to the wall in front of him and took down a set of keys hanging on a hook.

"Give Phil and Bob a call and tell them I'm on my way."

He drove onto the blacktopped perimeter road used by walkers and runners. The road was just wide enough to accommodate a car, but they were not allowed except for campus service vehicles.

Dawn was breaking behind the distant mountains to the east with the promise of a sunny day. After Wesson had driven about a mile he could see four police cruisers up ahead. Three were the campus patrol cars and one belonged to Sgt. Jones. Wesson pulled up next to the other cars and got out. There was a semi-circle of five men standing between the west edge of the path and a shallow ditch alongside. Wesson walked up to Sgt. Jones.

"What'd we have here, Bobby?"

"Well, we've got us a DB," said Jones.

"*Hey*! Who's minding the store?" Wesson called out to the patrol officers.

"Aw, we just stopped by ta see if we could help," said one of the officers.

"Well, thanks for the help, now get back on patrol," said Wesson. "Your shift isn't over yet."

The officers of patrols 1 and 2 got into their cars and left. Phil Owens of patrol 3 remained at the scene, because he had been collecting information from the young man who found the body. Using his flashlight in the dim early morning light, Wesson could see the body was a young blonde woman in white shorts and top. It looked like she had just been playing tennis. She was face down in the ditch half filled with water.

"Who found her?" asked Wesson.

"I did," said Daryl Johnson.

"When?"

"About an hour ago," said the young man.

"What were you doing here?"

Johnson was stung by what he thought was an accusing question.

"Look, I run on this path every morning."

"He's our quarterback," said Officer Owens.

"Oh, sure," said Wesson. "I thought I recognized you."

Wesson looked at Johnson for a moment, and then said, "When are we going to start winning some games?"

That really threw Johnson who became speechless.

Then Wesson asked, "Do you know this girl?"

"I don't know. I can't see her face."

"Well, you will when the coroner gets here."

Chapter 3
Coroner

Wesson went to his cruiser and pulled out the black bag. He rifled through it until he found a collapsed tripod and digital camera. He set up the tripod, attached the camera, and took several pictures of the body from different angles. He then took a shot of Johnson.

"Don't worry, Daryl. This is my way of taking notes of the scene."

"Phil, why don't you go back on patrol, but stick around in the office after your shift. I might need you when the coroner gets here. Sarge, go on home. I'll cover the rest of the shift."

Both men got into their cars and left.

"Daryl, let's take a seat in my car while we wait."

They both got into the front seat of Wesson's cruiser. He started the engine and turned on the heater to take off the morning chill.

"It's shaping up to be a gorgeous day," said Wesson, as he watched the sun climb higher into the sky. To the southeast they could see Mount Rainier, with its northern slopes reflecting the morning light as if it were made of gold. The western side was still in darkness.

"How can you do that?" asked Daryl.

"Do what?"

"Talk about the weather and be so unaffected about a dead girl only a few feet away?"

Daryl couldn't know how the detective really felt, or how anxieties raged within him. He had learned to put on an act as though he were in a play, and that he could walk away from the scene he was in anytime he wanted. His psychologist, Annie Alanson, had helped him learn to do this when he was a student, some years earlier.

"I freak-out when I take exams," he had complained to her. "My heart starts pounding, I break into a sweat and I think I'm dying."

"Well, that's easy to cure," said Annie. "All you have to do is get up from your desk and walk out of the room."

"I *can't* do that," he cried. "I'd flunk the course."

"But, your anxiety would go away."

It was then he realized he could escape his fears anytime he wanted by just walking away from them. On the other hand, he was now emboldened to endure his anxieties longer, finish his exams, improve his grade and earn his degree.

Wesson thought about Daryl's question for a minute and then asked, "What should I do?"

"I don't know," replied the young man. "Maybe show some sorrow. What about her parents? They're going to be devastated."

Wesson nodded and then asked, "You're the team quarterback, right?"

"Yeah."

"Who are you playing against next Saturday?"

"USC."

"Are they good?"

"They're leading the conference. They haven't lost a game."

"Have we lost any games?"

"A couple."

"When you go out on the field next Saturday and you see over 70,000 fans who expect you to play a perfect game, and then you see your opponent's linemen who look like Mack trucks, will your knees turn to water, and will you shake like a leaf?"

"No."

"Why not?"

"Because, if I let it get to me, I couldn't play."

"So, you and I aren't so different, are we?"

"Maybe not."

"What's your major?" asked Wesson.

"Sociology."

"Yeah, mine too. Are you taking it because it's easy?"

"No."

"I did. But then I took a criminology course from Michael Hunter, and that changed my life."

"Really, I'm taking that class, now."

"After I took that class, I knew exactly what I wanted to do, and I've never been sorry. What could be more interesting than human behavior?"

They spent the time talking about almost everything. Wesson learned a few things about football, and Johnson learned a few things about criminology and criminal types. In a while Wesson saw in his rearview mirror one of the police cruisers coming toward them followed by a green panel van.

"Well, it looks like they're here," he said as they got out of the car.

The two vehicles stopped and Wesson walked up to the van, and talked to a young man and woman.

"The body is right over there in the ditch," he said pointing.

They moved the van beside the ditch and got out. The two went to the rear of the van, opened the back doors and pulled out a gurney. As the man positioned the stretcher alongside the body, the young woman walked up to Wesson.

"Are you the officer in charge?" she asked.

"Yes."

"Anyone touch the body?"

"No."

"Can I get your name?" she asked as she opened a notebook.

"Here, take my card," said Wesson as he pulled one out of his pocket.

"Do you think this is a homicide?"

"I think so. We'll see when you turn her over."

"I see you had a camera set up. Will you provide us with copies?"

"Sure."

She seemed satisfied and joined her partner as they figured out the best way to turn the body over and put it on the gurney. Wesson, Johnson and the new officer on the scene, Mike Frizzon, stood next to each other as they watched.

"You're gonna have to get your feet wet," said Wesson.

The man and woman had to step into the ankle deep water in the ditch. He took hold of the body's arms near the shoulder, and she took hold of the legs. Rigor had set in so they could turn her over quite easily. Now they would be able to see the front of her body and face.

Dave Larson

"*Oh, my God!*" cried the woman as she dropped the legs and stumbled backward. The man too, dropped the arms and fell backward on to his butt, into the water. Wesson put his hand to his face and Daryl Johnson slumped to the ground as he nearly fainted. Officer Frizzon quickly turned and walked away.

Chapter 4
Professor Hunter

George Wesson walked along a brick path on the upper campus quadrangle, or "The Quad," on his way to the Behavioral Sciences Building to see his mentor, Professor Michael Hunter.

He smiled to himself as he remembered the story behind the brick pathways. It was in the 1960s, long before he became a student, that the Quad was a long rectangle lawn separating four halls, two on each side. Students would take short cuts, making dirt paths between the buildings. Eventually, the paths would become muddy and slick during rainy days. The Grounds Department was going to pave them with blacktop until the students found out. They wanted the paths to be paved with brick and threatened to raise hell if they weren't. They held sit-ins, rallies and almost went on strike before the Grounds Department relented.

After entering the building, Wesson walked down a hallway until he came to the open door of Hunter's outer office. The professor was talking to his administrative assistant when he looked up and saw his old student.

"Hi, George, "he said warmly, as he reached out his right hand.

Every time they met, Wesson could not help but glance at the professor's gloved left hand.

"Good to see you again, Michael," he replied with a smile.

They were good friends, and on a first name basis since Wesson had been in grad-school.

"Get yourself a cup of coffee and come on in to my office," said Hunter.

There was a coffee pot on a counter next to the secretary's desk. Wesson selected a mug hanging from a peg board above the bar and filled it. Then he followed the professor into the office.

"Have a seat," said Hunter, offering the detective a chair in front of his desk.

"How are things in the Campus Police world?" asked Hunter. "Do you still like your job?"

"Oh, very much," said Wesson. "Yesterday, I caught a kid who'd been stealing lunches from the coat racks in the HUB (Husky Union Building)."

"Sounds exciting," teased Hunter.

"Well, it was for him."

"What did you do with him?"

"I wrote a summary of what he did, and sent it to his dean with a recommendation the kid should be kicked out."

"What a heavy. You'd have this poor kid kicked out of school for stealing a lunch?" said the professor shaking his head in disapproval.

"Not lunch, but lunches. He'd been getting away with it for weeks. Michael, I know your philosophy of letting first offenders off with only a lecture, and then later after he shows up in prison for another more serious crime, you want to reform him by keeping him locked up with hardened criminals. It's like sending him to Criminal Methods 101."

Wesson and Hunter had this same discussion every time they got together. Each thought his method of punishing criminals was the right one.

"And, *your* method would be to cane him for a minor offense without giving him a second chance."

"It works in Singapore," said Wesson.

"Providing he wasn't first hung for some other minor crime."

Wesson smiled and then said, "This isn't why I'm here. I need to talk to you about something."

"You sound so serious."

"Do you mind if I close the door?"

Hunter looked surprised. "Go ahead."

Wesson got up from his chair and stepping to the door he checked the outer office and saw no one. Even the secretary was away from her desk. He closed the door and returned to his chair.

Dr. Hunter was waiting for some kind of bombshell.

The detective gathered his thoughts, and then said, "We had a homicide on campus last night."

"Oh?" said Hunter, expecting more.

"This is the first one, ever."

"How are you handling it? Are you calling in outside agencies?"

"No. I don't want to because they're shorthanded, and I don't think they'd do as good a job as we could. The chief won't be in until this afternoon, and I'm not sure of what he's going to say when I see him."

"You mean about bringing in someone else."

"Right. If someone other than the Campus Police gets involved, the media will get a hold of it and it'll be a circus. Just like the time we arrested the sports director of one of our TV stations for lewd behavior in the stadium restroom, and instead of handling it ourselves, we turned it over to SPD."

"Boy *that* turned into a fiasco didn't it?" said Hunter.

"Exactly. For weeks after, we had reporters and TV cameramen running rampant across the campus looking for a story."

"I remember that. The regents were really ticked-off with the publicity," laughed Hunter.

"Now, I'm in a tough spot. The Chief will think I'm not experienced enough to work the case. I want to show him a plan that will give him confidence."

"What would that be?"

"That you will be on my investigation team."

Hunter's eyes widened, "*Me*? You want *me* to help you?"

"Yes."

"To help you find a killer?"

"Yes."

"Why do you think I can help you?" asked Hunter. "My interests have been with criminal behavior, not crime solving."

"Let me show you some pictures of the crime scene."

Wesson pulled out a manila envelope from his inside sport coat pocket, and gave it to Hunter. His curiosity piqued, he opened the envelope. The pictures he saw caused him to cringe. He looked at each photo with its perspective.

"Have you ever seen anything like this before?" asked Wesson.

Hunter took several seconds of looking at the photos, before he answered.

"Yes. Yes I have."

"Do you have any idea of the kind of person we're looking for?"

By the grimacing expression on Hunter's face, Wesson could tell he was deeply affected.

Without looking up, he said, "Yes, I know the kind of person you're looking for."

Chapter 5
Chief Meyer

"Come on, Chief, be reasonable! I can handle this case!" cried Wesson.

It was after two o'clock in the afternoon and Chief Meyer had just come in after spending the earlier part of the day having a root canal done. He was livid to find out about the first recorded murder on campus, and he didn't hear a thing about it until he found Wesson camped in his office. Even with the office door closed, everyone could hear him screaming through the walls.

"Why in God's name didn't you call me as soon as you found the body?" the Chief shouted.

"But *Chief,* I knew you had this dental appointment this morning, and I couldn't see laying this on you, too," said Wesson.

"Don't give me that! You saw a chance to try and set yourself up as the big shot detective on what you think will become a big story."

"*No*! I wouldn't do that!"

"And, then you go behind my back and try to get some *communist* to help you."

"*Communist*? What'd ya mean communist?" shouted Wesson.

"Well, he's a Socialist professor, isn't he?"

"He's a Sociology professor! He's a criminologist, for God's sake!"

"Communist, Sociologist! They're all the same to me, and why you went to him, I'll never know."

"Look, Chief, this is important to me. I know I can handle it."

"Have you ever handled a murder case before?"

"Of course not. This is the first for any of us."

"That's why I think we should turn this over to SPD."

"Aw, Chief, don't do *that*! Give me a chance. This is our golden opportunity to show we can handle anything that comes our way."

Chief Meyer reflected on that for a moment.

"This would be a full time job. How are you going handle the rest of your work?

"You mean to catch starving students who are stealing lunches, or those too lazy to walk and steal bicycles? I think Danny can handle that stuff for a while."

"I'm gonna call this Commie professor and talk to him, and then I wanna talk to you again. Now, get outta my office!"

When Wesson opened the door he found some of the staff had obviously been listening to the tirades and were now backing away. This amused him because he was the only one who would stand up to the Chief.

He went into the break room and poured a cup of coffee. His partner, Danny Smith, was sitting at the table telling war stories to one of the patrol officers.

"So, I'm standing back, watchin' the lunch bag I'd just planted on the shelf above the coat rack, when I saw this kid come along and take it."

Oh, yeah?" said the patrol officer.

"Yeah! Then I introduce myself to the kid, and ask him if he made his own lunch. He sez, 'yeah'. So I sez, 'What kind of sandwiches did you make?' And he sez, 'Tuna'. Then we open the bag and there's nothing there but wadded up paper. Then I put the cuffs on him."

"*Wow!* What an exciting story," said the patrol officer mockingly, as he finished his coffee and got up from his chair. "You guy's sure have it rough." He was laughing as he walked out to his patrol car.

Then Danny let out a long sigh, realizing he'd just made a fool of himself for the umpteenth time.

Wesson felt sorry for him, realizing he sold him a promising bill of goods that didn't measure up.

"Danny, don't cast your pearls before swine."

He knew what Wesson meant. Don't talk about your job unless you have something to talk about.

"Oh, while you were out this morning, a call came in from the manager of the HUB," said Danny. "He wants you to call him back."

"About what?"

"I don't know."

Wesson was a little peeved that his partner didn't take the initiative to find out what he wanted.

He went to his office and found a post-it-note on top of his desk, with a phone number. He dialed the number and a woman's voice answered, "HUB manager's office."

"This is Detective Wesson calling back."

"Just a moment, please."

Then, a man's voice came on the line, "Hello, this is James Wilson."

"This is Detective Wesson of the University Police."

"Oh, thank you for returning my call. I've got a problem here."

"No one stealing lunches, I hope."

"No, nothing like that. I've been getting threats from someone who is probably psychotic."

"Really? What's he saying to you?"

"Well, for starters, he thinks I'm the football coach. Every time the football team loses a game, he blames me."

"You must be getting a lot of threats from him."

"Yeah, I have. But last week he said he'll kill me if we lose the next game."

"Let's see, our next game is tomorrow with USC. I think you're in a world of hurt."

"What should I do?"

"Do you know his name?"

"I believe his name is Dick Crow."

"You're right. He's been on the campus for years. He's about sixty years, old and he always wears a baseball cap with a big letter 'W' on it".

"That's the guy," said Wilson.

"OK. Do you and your staff usually work on Saturdays?"

"I usually come in on game Saturdays because it gets pretty active."

"Well, this Saturday, I want you to take the day off."

"What will you do?"

"Don't worry about it."

"Will you need a key for my office?"

"No, we have one here in our office."

"Well, OK. No one is going to get hurt, are they?"

"I hope not. I'll talk to you on Monday," said Wesson.

"OK. Bye."

"Bye," said Wesson, and then he hung up the phone.

The Chief opened his office door and called out, "*Wesson!*"

"*Yeah?*" Wesson hollered back from his office.

"Get your partner and come back in here!"

Danny left the break room when he heard the Chief and met Wesson at the office door. After they entered, Chief Meyers closed the door and then sat down at his desk. Danny became nervous and fidgety as the Chief gazed directly at him.

"Danny, do you think you can handle your job for a while without your partner's help?"

"Uh, sure. Yeah."

Then Chief Meyer shifted his gaze on Wesson.

"George, why didn't you tell me who this professor of yours *is?*"

"Uh, I thought I...." stammered Wesson.

"Why, this guy's a famous criminologist. Even was the warden at the McNeil pen."

"I know, I...."

"Famous for classifying types of criminals."

Wesson could only roll his eyes and shake his head. He wasn't going to get credit for anything. Then he asked, "So you called him then?"

"Yes. He said he'd be glad to help us on this one. He said he knows you, and would be glad to have you work for him."

"*What?*"

"I'm hiring him as a consultant, and giving him a free hand over everything and full privileges as a commander. You will be his assistant. You'll work directly for him until this thing gets cleared up."

"*No! No*, I will *not!*" Wesson shouted. "This is *my* case! He's supposed to be helping *me!*"

"Why would he work for you?" Chief Meyer yelled back. Danny was looking for some place to hide.

The Chief continued, "Look, he's older and more experienced than you and he's smarter than you. What kind of fool would I look like to put you in charge over *him?* Come on, George, use your head!"

"What if Hunter decides to do everything himself, and I don't have any work to do?"

"Then you come back here and help out Danny?"

"I suppose you're gonna tell me Danny's no longer my assistant and that I'm his assistant."

"Yeah," the Chief said as he lit his lighter to fire up his pipe.

"I give up!" said a very angry Wesson as he banged open the office door against its stop and stormed out.

Chapter 6
The Defective Detective

Detective Lieutenant George Wesson sat alone in his office wondering what would become of him. What if they can't find the killer? Will he lose his job? The stress was gradually awaking the anxiety monster that resided deep within him.

He was a complicated man. Around others, he put on a convincing display of self-assuredness, but inside he was burning with self-doubts and anxiety. His greatest fear was that his weakness may someday boil to the surface for all to see. He was afraid he might be harboring a mental disease that someday would cost him his job, his marriage and even his life.

I'd better call Hunter, he thought.

He picked up the phone and dialed a number.

"Sociology Department," answered a woman's voice.

"This is Lt. Wesson from the University Police. May I please speak with Dr. Hunter?"

There was a brief ringing of an extension, then....

"Hello, Michael Hunter,"

"Michael, this is George."

"George! I was just going to call you. Has anyone talked with this girl's parents?"

"I haven't. I don't even know who she is."

"Hmmm. Well, I've got all of her personal information from the coroner and admissions office. I'll fax it over to you. After you get it, why don't you give them a call? Then call the University public relations office and have them contact the local media. Tell them we'll have a news conference in the Administration Building lobby at ten o'clock tomorrow morning."

"Do you want me to be there, too?"

"Of course I want you there. You're going to hold it."

"Uh, maybe you should do it, Michael."

Hunter was silent for a moment, and then said, "No. You're going to hold it. Come here at eight o'clock tomorrow morning and I'll help you prepare for it." Then he hung up the phone.

Wesson didn't feel good. He felt like he used to just before taking a final exam. He could hear Patrol Sgt. Walt Franklin talking to someone at the main desk.

The detective stuck his head out of his office door and called out, "Hey, Walt! Ya got a second?" Franklin looked up and saw it was Wesson calling him. He quickly ended his conversation with the desk officer, and then started down the hall to Wesson's office. "What ya got, George?"

"I wanna ask you somethin'. You've worked on other police forces, right?"

"Sure," said the older, more experienced officer. "I was on the Tacoma Police Department. for fifteen years. Why?"

"You ever work on a homicide?"

"Sure."

"Ever work on a case where the victim is from outta town?"

"Yeah."

"So how did ya tell the victim's family?"

"Oh. We'd call their local police department and give them the information, and then they'd send someone over to tell them."

"OK. Thanks."

"No problem," said the Sergeant as he turned and left.

Wesson could hear the fax running. He stepped to the machine and saw the sheets of paper sliding out of it. When it finished printing, he picked them up and took them to his desk.

He looked for the name.

Carol Jones. Age? Twenty. A junior. From? Lynnwood, Washington. "*Oh no*! Why couldn't she have been from someplace like California?" he said aloud. Actually, Lynnwood was only five miles from Edmonds, where Wesson lived. He could have easily driven there to deliver the news himself.

What should I do? he thought.

Then he looked up the Lynnwood Police Department's telephone number and dialed. It wasn't even long distance.

"Lynnwood Police, Officer Kimmel," answered a male voice.

"Uh, Officer Kimmel, this is Lt. Wesson from the University of Washington P.D. Homicide Division."

There was a second of silence, and then, "*Homicide*? You guys have a Homicide Division?"

"Well, it's small. There are only two of us staffing it right now. But we're expecting to grow."

"Is this a joke? This isn't some kind of fraternity prank, is it?"

Wesson could feel rivulets of cold sweat running down his back, as he struggled to sound professional and knowledgeable.

"No. Really, I'm serious."

"OK. What do you want?"

"What?"

"Look, you called me. What do *you* want?"

"Oh! Well we had a homicide on the campus last night. It was a girl from Lynnwood. We'd like to have you notify the parents for us. I can fax you the information."

"When did you find the body?"

"Five o'clock this morning. I thought we could let you guys do that out of professional courtesy. We wouldn't want to intrude on your turf."

"You found the body almost *eleven* hours ago, and you're just getting around to breaking the news to the parents?" Officer Kimmel asked incredulously. "No wonder you don't want to tell them."

"Well, we got pretty busy with this thing. You know, with only two of us and all...."

"Let me talk to your chief."

Wesson's mouth was so dry he could hardly speak. "Uh, well," he stammered, "he's not in right now. Besides I'm on special assignment with this case, so I don't work for the chief right now."

"You said there were two of you working on this," said Kimmel.

"Yeah, I've got a consultant helping me."

"What's his name?"

"Dr. Michael Hunter."

"Did you say, Doctor?"

"Yeah. Professor Hunter. He's a rather famous criminologist."

"And he works for *you*?"

"Well, we're really kind of equals."

"What's his phone number?"

"Oh, I'm sure he's teaching a class."

"Then I'll call him when he's out of class."

Wesson fished out a piece of paper from his middle desk drawer with Hunter's phone number and read it to Officer Kimmel.

"Well, I'll talk to you again, soon," said Wesson.

"I hope not," replied Kimmel, who then hung up. Wesson sat at his desk still holding the handset to his ear.

"I really screwed that up," he thought out loud.

He then called the Public Relations Office, and told them of the next day's press conference. Just then, Danny stuck his head in the doorway.

"Did ya call that guy from the HUB?"

"What guy?"

"The manager guy?"

"Oh, yeah. What are you doing tomorrow?"

"I'm going to the game. Why, you got something?"

"What time are the games usually over?"

"About four o'clock."

"OK, I want you to meet me at the HUB manager's office at three o'clock."

"Hey, that means I'll miss the fourth quarter."

"So, what? They'll be losing by then anyway."

As soon as Danny left, Wesson's telephone rang.

"Lt. Wesson."

"George? It's Michael. I just got a call from the Lynwood Police Department."

"Yeah, I figured you'd be hearing from them," said Wesson apologetically.

"Well, hear me out, George. I don't think it was such a bad idea for you to ask them to call on the parents.

"Really?"

"Yeah. I'm sorry I put the burden on you. I should have realized your department had no experience in something like this. Anyway, they've agreed to talk to the parents, and they'll take grief counselors.

Chapter 7
President Denney

At eight o'clock Saturday morning, Detective Lt. Wesson walked into the Sociology Department reception office. Seeing no one else around, he continued down the inner hallway to where the faculty members reside. The door to Hunter's office was open and he could see the professor hunched over his desk, as he was poring over some items from an open file.

"Ahem!" Wesson cleared his throat.

Hunter turned around and saw the detective standing in his doorway. "Oh, hello, George," he said with a smile. "Come on in and have a seat."

Wesson expected Hunter to be angry after yesterday, but, to his surprise, he was cordial. He sat down in a wooden chair in front in the professor's desk. Hunter was wearing casual clothes and seemed relaxed. Wesson, on the other hand, was spiffy in his slacks, sport coat and polished shoes. No tie though. He always avoided wearing a tie.

"Look, Michael, I'm really sorry about yesterday."

Hunter cut him off. "George, let's forget about that right now. You have to get ready to address about a dozen people from the news media. What are you going to tell them?"

"I'll tell them when we found the body, and where, and how viciously she was attacked, and I'll tell them how we'll let nothing stand in our way to find the person responsible for this."

Hunter cringed a bit. "I don't think you'll have to be that passionate, George. Just give them the simple facts. You don't want to give up too much information. You don't want to tip your hand to the killer."

"I've never had an occasion to do anything like this before. I don't know how to begin."

"I said I'd help you out on this," said Hunter. "I have it all written out for you. All you have to do is read it."

"That's all?"

"Well, they'll be asking some questions after you read the statement. Just make sure all of the answers to their questions stay within the framework of the statement. Whatever you do, don't try to wing it. Let them think they are getting more information from you by reformatting the same information over again."

Hunter gave Wesson a single printed sheet.

"Why do I have to do this?" asked Wesson. "Why can't you do this? You're really in charge."

"*Look*," said Hunter impatiently. "Just get us through this one thing today. Do you think you could do that much?"

Wesson now realized how worried, frightened, unsure, incompetent and stupid he really was. When the chips were down, he knew he was really a fake. He liked the image of being a cop, and carrying the badge and gun. But, right now the wind had been taken out of his sails. He felt ashamed and alone, almost to the point of tears. He looked into Hunter's face and managed to squeak, "Yes."

"I'm sure you'll do a good job, George. Now let's walk over to the administration building and talk to President Denney, before the media people get here."

"The school's president's gonna be there?"

"Yeah, he has to convince the public this is a safe school, and the incident was just an anomaly. He doesn't want people to think we have a serial killer running loose here."

They went out of the building, across the quad, past the flagpole plaza, and on to a brick walkway that led to the main entrance of a large Gothic building that was festooned with spires and gargoyles. They opened the massive bronze doors, so well balanced they pivoted with ease. Every window in the building was an assembly of leaded glass pieces. This building could have rivaled many cathedrals in the world. It was hard to believe only day to day office business activities were done here by people with computers, telephones, paper and pen - the same activities that take place in all other office buildings throughout the world. But, this building, gave the impression of elegance and holiness.

They stepped into the lobby and on to a polished marble floor. Wesson could see a podium had been erected, with electrical extension and microphone cords running off into the distance. The University President, Emil Denney, was standing in the middle of the lobby floor, with his hands in his pockets, talking to another man. The man left and Denney turned around and saw Hunter and Wesson heading his way. He gave them a big smile stretched out his right hand to greet them.

"Michael, I'm glad you're here," said Denney as they shook hands.

"Emil, this is the young man I've been telling you about, Officer Wesson."

"Happy to meet you, son," said Denney as they shook hands.

Wesson smiled and nodded.

Young man? Son? Wesson thought to himself. *What is this?*

"Let's step into this conference room for a little chat before people start coming in," said Denney.

They went into a nearby room, turned on the lights, and sat at a table. Wesson had seen Denney several times, but had never spoken to him. He doubted if the man had ever noticed him.

"Michael tells me you were recently promoted from a patrol officer," said Denney as he regarded Wesson with a smile.

"Yes, sir. About six months ago."

"And, you were Michael's student?"

"Yeah," responded Wesson.

George watched his smiling face. Denney had mostly white hair and a small white mustache, and like Hunter, the President also wore wire rimmed glasses.

"You know, George, this is a *great* university. Very prestigious. Students come here from all over the United States and the rest of the world. We have one of the best foreign student programs. Our graduate, medical, law and arts and science schools have no equal."

Wesson nodded his head in agreement, not knowing what else to do.

Denney leaned back in his chair and looked over Wesson head, fixing his gaze on the wall, as he carefully chose his next words.

"And now we have this *little* problem."

Did he say little? thought Wesson.

Almost as if he were reading Wesson's mind, Denney tried to correct his comment.

"I don't really mean *little*. There will be people who will see this news conference on TV who will think this happens more than it does, and it could snowball to the point where enrollment could be affected."

"So, you see, George," said Hunter, "you have an important part, just by making a short statement to the news media."

"Will Chief Meyer be here?"

"No," said Denney. "We've decided to take it out of his hands entirely and let you and Michael handle this."

"Oh," said Wesson, with surprise. *Why wouldn't the chief be here?* he thought.

"George, you've got a degree in Sociology with studies in Criminology. Chief Meyer worked his way up through the ranks, and has never attended college. He's a good administrator and police officer, but he's never handled a case quite like this one".

Neither have I, thought Wesson.

Denney went on.

"The most important aspect of this case, George, is we have to control all of the information surrounding it. We are going to give one, and only one news conference, and then we'll let things return to normal. When we finally arrest the perpetrator, then and only then, will we have any more to say to the media."

"Uh, Dr. Denney, why the secrecy?" asked Wesson. "If we keep the media informed, maybe someone will come forward with some information."

Emil Denney glanced at Michael Hunter, who was standing nearby, looking down at the floor.

"With news like this, George, can you imagine what it will do to the school's reputation?"

"Well yeah, but…."

"*Listen*, you just do as you're told. I don't want to hear any more about it!" Denney snapped.

Wesson was shaken by the sudden fit of anger thrown at him by the university president. He was beginning to wonder if he was making one blunder after another, and if he was treading blindly into uncharted areas.

Chapter 8
Press Conference

At ten o'clock, President Denney, followed by Wesson, stepped into the blaze of lights, and in front of the cameras. Wesson stood back as a serious looking university president faced the crowd of cameramen and reporters. All of the local TV stations were accounted for, as were the two major newspapers. Some of the small neighborhood newspapers, and even the university students' paper, "The Daily," were also represented.

"Good morning," announced Denney.

"We are saddened to announce the death of one of our students. We don't yet know the cause of death. Lt. Wesson, of the University Police is investigating. He'll now provide you with the details as we know them."

President Denney stepped aside and Wesson replaced him at the podium. He placed the single sheet of paper on the lectern that Hunter had given him. He tried to read the notes written by Hunter, and he would have to stay within the boundaries of their scope, but with the glare of lights and his myopia, he couldn't see a thing. He decided to tell the story in the first person. It was either that, or it would be the shortest news conference given by anyone.

"Around five-thirty yesterday morning," he began, "I was awakened by a call from the desk officer who reported to me of the finding of a DB on the campus."

"What's a DB?" called out a voice from behind the glare.

"Oh, that's a dead body in police talk. When I got to the office, I learned it was found on the perimeter road."

"The what?" asked another voice from somewhere on the floor.

"The perimeter road? You know, it's a road that goes around the edge of the campus." Seeing his answer sufficed, Wesson continued. "So when I got there, I saw the DB lying in a ditch."

"Was the person who found the body still there when you arrived at the scene?" asked a voice.

"Yes, he was."

"Did you arrest him?"

"No. Why would I do that?"

"Maybe he's the murderer."

"We don't know if she was murdered. We're waiting to hear from the medical examiner," said Wesson.

Actually, he knew without question the girl was murdered, most hideously, but that information was outside of the boundaries set by Hunter and Denney.

"Now, I've told you about all of the information we currently have. I'll be glad to answer questions."

"Did you examine the body?" asked a voice?"

"I made a cursory examination when the body was removed."

"Did you see evidence of violence?"

"I'm afraid our time is up," said Denney, as he replaced Wesson at the podium. "Thank you all for coming."

On that note, the camera lights were turned off, and the reporters started milling around and talking amongst themselves. Wesson was still standing near the podium when a young woman came up to him.

"Hi. My name's Lisa. I'm a reporter for The Daily, the school newspaper."

"Hi, Lisa."

"I'm a friend of Daryl Johnson."

"Who?"

"He found the body."

"Oh yeah, and this afternoon, he'll be leading our team down the field to another defeat."

"He told me the girl was murdered."

"Do you know him pretty well?"

"We've been going together."

"Would you give him a message from me?"

"Sure."

"Tell him it is very important he doesn't talk to anyone else about finding the body. Tell him I wouldn't want to see something happen to him."

"Are you threatening him?"

"No. Not me, but I've got a bad feeling. Tell him to call me when he can. Here's my card, in case he threw away the first one I gave him."

Hunter was waiting near the outside door of the lobby. The detective joined him, and together they walked to the Behavioral Sciences Building.

After a few minutes, Hunter asked, "Who was the young woman you were talking to?"

"Just a reporter."

"Be sure you share with me everything you know, or have questions about," said Hunter.

They arrived at the building which was still empty. Hunter sat down at his desk and the detective again sat on the chair facing the professor.

"What did you think about the news conference?" asked the detective.

Hunter smiled and said, "You did a good job, George."

"You gotta be kidding! I thought I did an awful job. I feel like a stupid ass."

"Why?"

"Why? Because I looked like a clown up there. I had such little information. I felt like a fool."

"Was that your fault?"

"*No*! You guys wouldn't let me say anything."

"George, when you see a news conference on TV, do you think it's to provide information or disinformation?"

"What? You mean you were having me lie to those people?"

"No. Not lie, George. We wanted you to give out as little information as possible, and you did a great job."

Wesson was speechless for a moment, and then asked, "Why? What was the purpose of it?"

"All of those members of the media have noted they were here for a news conference about finding a body on the campus. With so little information there probably will be no follow up. It gives us time without interference. No one can accuse us of sand bagging information when the conference is on record. We've notified the public."

"There's a reason for this?"

Dr. Michael Hunter looked at Wesson as he sat at his desk and gave a deep sigh. "Think back when you were a student in my class."

"OK."

"Do you remember the different subtypes of killers?"

"I think so. There was the situation killer who was facing a threat from someone like a blackmailer. There was the guy that kills in the commission of a crime, the contract killer, the paranoid, the sociopath who kills for pleasure, the ...."

"Stop right there," said Hunter. "Of the ones you just mentioned, what type do you think killed that girl?"

"It was probably a sociopath."

"Why do you think so?"

"Well, because of the brutality. It looked like the work of an animal."

"Do you remember from the class, I said a sociopath killer often leaves his signature?"

"Yeah, but I wasn't looking for anything like that. What was his signature?"

"Didn't you notice that the girl was missing her *left hand*?"

"What?" said Wesson, as he now found his stare locked on Hunter's gloved left hand.

Chapter 9
The Alpha Male

Detective Lt. George Wesson was at a loss for words. What was his friend, mentor, and now superior, telling him? He stood up from his chair, his eyes now shifting from "the claw" to Hunter's face.

"What are you saying, Michael? You really know who this guy *is*, don't you? Does this have something to do with the loss of your own hand?"

"Yes."

Wesson slowly sat back down again, wide eyed and stunned.

"Tell me, Michael. Tell me what happened."

In Wesson's coat pocket was a devise sensitive enough to record conversations within a ten foot radius. It was a high-tech replacement for a note pad and pencil. He slipped his hand into his pocket and turned it on.

As Wesson sat quietly waiting, Hunter collected his thoughts.

"You know, I became the acting warden for one year at McNeil Island."

"Yes. You told our class. It was when you made the observations for defining criminal types."

"A year before that I tried to get permission from the existing warden to let me make observations and take blood samples, but he wasn't interested."

"What was his name?" asked Wesson.

"His name was, Holdem, Will Holdem."

"What happened to him?"

"No one knows. He just vanished. Then, Governor Headmann, asked me to finish out Holdem's contract that had a year left. This was my chance to make the survey on criminal types. When I took over, I soon realized I couldn't collect data and blood samples without help."

"So, did you get help from prison guards?"

"No. I had a better idea than that. By making my own observations, and querying the prison staff, I was able to identify the inmate who had the greatest influence. Both the inmates and the staff called him the '*Alpha Male*' or *AM*. Even he preferred to go by the name, AM."

"What was his real name?"

"I don't know. I didn't want to know any of their names. I didn't want to humanize them. I wanted to look at them only as data."

"What was the 'Alpha Male' like?"

"He was a large powerful middle eastern man, about 220 pounds with a short black beard. He was a loner. He had no friends and didn't seem to want any. The other inmates were afraid of him. He seemed to make them do whatever he wanted. I never saw him perform any act of violence but you knew he could in a heartbeat."

"How old was he?"

"It was hard to tell. Somewhere around 30, I think. I wanted to interview him, so I asked the staff to set up a room with a table and two chairs. After the inmates were locked in their cells for the evening, I had the Captain of the Guards take him to a room. When I entered he was sitting on a wooden chair with his bare feet shackled to the floor, and his wrists strapped to a heavy oak table. When I asked the captain to remove his restraints, he took me aside.

***

"I don't think we should do that, Dr. Hunter. Have you seen this man's rap sheet?"

"No, but it's very important I have no information about these men. It could invalidate the study."

He then nodded to the other guards and they removed the restraints. AM didn't move. He sat perfectly still as though he were still restrained. The captain said he would keep a couple of men outside the door. I agreed and they left, closing the door behind them.

I went to the table and sat down on the chair facing AM. Our eyes met, but his gaze seemed to pass right through me. I tried to introduce myself.

"Hello, I'm Michael Hunter."

"What do you want?"

"Well, I'd just like to get to know you."

"Why?"

That's all he said, with no emotion, and still looking through me.

"I'm the new warden here."

"I know."

I had a chance now to see this man up close. His most prominent facial features were his large hooked nose, and dark eyes. He had the black stubble of a beard, and his head was as bald and slick as a billiard ball. His huge frame was muscular from working out. He looked immensely strong.

"Where is your home?"

"Egypt."

"Are you a Muslim?"

This time he stirred.

"What do you want?"

"I want you to help me on a research project."

Now he was becoming alive. He started looking around the room, like he just realized where he was.

"What kind of research project?"

"It's a study to describe the types of inmate characteristics."

"Will this make you rich?"

"No."

"Then why do this?"

"Maybe it will make me famous in my field."

"If I help you, what do I get?"

"What do you want?"

"I want *freedom*."

"I can't give you that."

Then suddenly his hands flew out and grabbed my coat lapels. He pulled me across the table until my face nearly touched his.

"I could *kill* you before the guard can open the door."

"*Please*! *Stop*! You're choking me!"

"Only if you give me freedom," he said.

***

Then he insisted I make my promise in writing. There was a wash basin in the room with paper towels. He got up from his chair and got a towel from the dispenser, and brought it back to the table. Before I went into the room with him, the guards took away a pen I had in my shirt pocket because it could be used as a weapon. But, I had another small pen attached to a key chain they let me keep. It was with that pen AM had me sign my life away. I promised him his freedom upon conclusion of the study. I put it in writing on that paper towel, and signed it. He folded it and stuffed it in his waist band. I knew there was nothing I could do to free him, and I'm certain he knew it too.

"So you didn't tell anyone about what happened?" asked Wesson.

"No. I felt pretty stupid about it. But, who could have blamed me for what I did. I was sure he would have killed me if I didn't do what he wanted."

"How did you get the data for your study?"

"My main concern was to get accurate data. It would be just like the inmates to try and con me. So, with help from the staff, I selected a viable random sample of inmates by their identification numbers."

"How large was the sample?"

"100."

"*Wow*! You interviewed 100 inmates?

"Yes."

"Did he help you?"

"Yes. I made a list of the inmate identification numbers to be interviewed and had the staff give it to him. He then spoke to each inmate on the list, and told them to be cooperative. Each inmate was brought into a room, one at a time. They were given a battery of both written and oral questions about their personalities and behaviors. Graduate students had helped me to formulate these questions, and we were sure they were the right ones to ask. The prison nurse drew a blood sample from each man.

"After I collected all of the information, I sent the data to the team of graduate students back in Seattle, and sent the blood samples to my home where they were stored in a refrigerator until my return. Then, I took the documentation and blood samples to Dr. Barnes for analysis."

"What were you expecting to find?"

"I expected to find the 'Superman' gene with the XYY chromosomes. I published my results and, as you know, it's available for anyone to read."

"Yes, I read your paper, Michael, and I was disappointed. I don't think you've proved your case. Not everyone with the 'Superman' gene appears to be a sociopath."

"It seems that way. I think I've got to repeat the study, but with a much larger sample."

"When did the riot take place?"

"About a week before my contract was up. Somehow the prisoners got out of their cells and burned their bedding. I went in with the guards, because I wanted to experience the disturbance firsthand."

"Weren't you afraid you'd meet up with AM?"

"He was supposed to be in a maximum secure cell block. I had him sent there because I was sure he'd kill me for lying to him. We were inching our way down a corridor in thick smoke when we were suddenly attacked, and I was separated from the guards. The next thing I knew, someone pulled a towel over my head and I was dragged out of the cell block. When they took the towel away, I found I was in the cell block kitchen and face to face with AM.

"He accused me of profiting from his work, and not paying him. I was so frightened I couldn't speak. Then he had two guys hold me and placed my left wrist on a chopping block. He grabbed a cleaver and chopped off my hand. I fell to the floor and passed out. Later, I woke up in the prison infirmary. Since then, I returned to the university. We've kept the incident out of the news. All that was reported was that there was a disturbance, not a full scale riot, and one prisoner escaped."

"So he got his freedom," commented Wesson. "Why did he kill the girl?"

"To let me know he was here. He's like a cat playing with a mouse. He wants to terrorize me. He enjoys it."

"How did he get out of the secured cell block?"

"He must own one of the staff members."

Wesson could hardly believe what Michael had just told him. Here was one of the world's greatest criminologists who was in league with the devil, all because he wanted to prove his theory about criminal types. The man was a genius, but unfortunately so was his pursuer.

"Michael, what are you going to do?"

"I don't know. I'm sure he's going to play games to terrorize me before he kills me. I'm not looking forward to his method. I've got to find him before he finds me."

Wesson's cell phone suddenly rang with a call from Danny.

"What's going on, Danny?"

"You're late," answered Danny. "It's ten past three."

"Sorry Danny. I got held up on something. Are you at the manager's office now?"

"Yeah, I just got here."

"OK, I'll be there in a few minutes."

"Roger," said Danny and hung up.

The Professor was still sitting behind the desk, gazing out of the window.

"Michael, I'm going to be gone for a while. Are you going to be all right?"

Hunter looked at him and smiled.

"Yeah, I'll be OK," he said. "Look, George, thanks for listening to me. I feel a lot better getting it off my chest. I hope you'll keep this between us."

"Don't worry, Michael. It'll stay in this room. Now I know what my real job is."

"What's that?"

"I'm your bodyguard."

Chapter 10
Mistaken Identity

The Husky Union Building was centrally located on the campus and its acronym, HUB, seemed to fit. It was a large brick structure that served the student body with lots of activities. In the basement there was a bowling alley and a game room with several pool tables. On the first floor there was a large cafeteria, a snack bar, several couches, and low tables where students could do their homework, or just sleep. On the second floor was a ballroom and administrative offices.

One of the offices belonged to the HUB manager, James Wilson. He had called the University Police saying his life had been threatened by a local character, Richard Crow, whom everyone thought to be harmless. Richard was well known to the police as a nuisance. He was about 60 years old and an avid football fan. He always wore a purple baseball cap with a golden 'W' on the front. He probably had been a student at the school in the distant past, but no one ever checked it out. Some of the officers who knew him would joke about his odd behavior, but not Wesson. To him, it was cruel and unprofessional to make fun of the man.

But, now Richard had crossed the line. He was no longer harmless because he had threatened to kill the HUB manager if the football team lost another game. In his mind he thought the manager, James Wilson, and the football coach were one and the same, or connected in some way. Richard spent a lot of time in the HUB and was always trying to talk to students who were busy studying, or reading. Apparently, he took notice of James, who was quite visible because of his job. One day Richard went up to James and asked who he was. When James told him he was the

HUB manager, Richard got it in his head that James was involved with the football team. He followed him to his office, and then every Saturday after that, he would plunk himself down in James' office and complain about the performance of the team. He was often asked to leave, sometimes by a patrolling officer, but every Saturday after a game, he'd come back again. Unhappily for James, the team this year had a losing season. So, a frustrated Richard now threatened to kill him if they lost one more game.

James was worried enough to call the police. Wesson told him to take the next game day off, and that he would take care of the problem. So, now the detective and his partner, Danny Smith, were arranging a trap for Richard. There wasn't much hope for the Huskies to win this game, as they were playing the USC Trojans who were leading the conference.

Wesson met Danny and produced a key. The office was small, with a desk and an upholstered chair next to it. There were also a couple of wooden chairs backed up to the side wall in front of the desk. Danny had put a small battery radio on the desk so they could hear the game.

"It should be a piece of cake to take this guy down," said Danny.

"Why do you think so?" responded Wesson as he made some minor adjustments to the furniture, assuring open space in front of the desk.

Danny was sitting in the swivel chair behind the desk, twirling it trying to make it go all the way around with one push of his foot.

"The guy's old. We should take him down in seconds."

"What if the old guy has a gun or a knife?"

Danny was now leaning back in the chair and looking out of the window behind the desk. It was beginning to rain.

"I wouldn't be afraid if he had a knife. A gun might be a problem though."

Wesson looked at him and laughed. Danny was only a few years younger than Wesson, but sometimes he behaved like a kid.

"OK, Danny, this is what we'll do. After the game is over, I want you to be sitting at the desk and keep your head down like you're working on something."

"Is there any special reason you want *me* at the desk?"

"He's never seen you before. He must have seen me five or six times. It probably wouldn't make any difference, I doubt if he will even notice you're not the manager, but keep your head down just in case."

"OK," said Danny.

"Now, I'll be standing outside of the office door, and we'll keep it open."

"Should I have my pistol out?"

"Yeah. Let's see. I know. Put this 'in' basket on the desk and lay the Glock on the desktop behind it. Then rest your right hand on the butt of the gun. Now, I've told you what he looks like, and you can't miss seeing his baseball cap with the 'W'. As soon as you see him, lower your head so he can't get a good look at your face."

"OK," said Danny nodding in agreement."

"Now, I'll be right outside the door. I'll come in right behind him and close the door. Without looking up, say, 'I'll be right with you Mr. Crow. Please have a seat.'"

"I'll sit down next to him and grab his arm and hold him. Then you slide out of your chair and help me cuff him. Does this sound like a plan?"

"Sounds good to me," said Danny.

"How's the game going?"

"Not so good," said Danny. "We're down 21 to zip with about two minutes to go in the fourth quarter. The announcer says it's raining hard, and not many people are left in the stands."

"Oh-oh! Maybe Richard gave up on the game early, too."

Before Wesson could turn around, he felt his presence.

"I told you I'd kill you if we lost again!" said a voice behind the detective. A chill ran up his back as he turned around in time to see Richard Crow, standing in the doorway, pulling a sawed-off, double barrel shotgun out from under his coat, and leveling it at the two officers.

Chapter 11
An Eventful Day

Time slowed to nearly a stop. Danny could feel his right hand on the butt of his gun, but couldn't seem to make it move. Wesson tried to move toward Richard, but he felt like his body was immersed in water. He launched himself from the floor with his right foot and leg. His body was stretched out to its full length following his extended right hand which was now sliding down the shotgun's barrels towards the firing hammers. He felt a stab of pain as the hammer of the left barrel was triggered, pinching the web of skin between his thumb and forefinger. His head and right shoulder collided with Richard's chest sending him backward. The right barrel of the shotgun fired its load harmlessly into the hall ceiling.

Wesson got to his knees straddling Richard who was flat on his back on the hall floor with his eyes wide open. Danny flew to Wesson's side with his 9mm Glock firmly in his hand.

"George, are you all right?" he excitedly asked.

"Yeah. He fired next to my ear. I can't hear a thing. Help me turn him over so you can get your cuffs on him."

"I dunno, George. He don't look too good. Is he breathing?"

Wesson put his face next to Richard's.

"I think he's got some breath in him. Help me roll him over."

The two officers were oblivious to the crowd of students that came running at the sound of the shot.

They rolled Richard on to his face and Danny used the cuffs he carried on his belt. Richard started struggling to Wesson's relief.

"I think he's OK. He must have been unconscious."

They pulled Richard to his feet. He was now shouting obscenities.

"Man, that was the first time I've ever stared down the bad end of a shotgun," said Danny.

"Me, too."

"Richard, what ya got in your pockets?" asked Danny as he began searching him. "Oh, here's some more shotgun shells."

Richard looked at Wesson's face and showed a flicker of remembrance.

"I know *you.* You're one of them police guys."

"Richard, why were you trying to shoot us?"

"I didn't know it was you guys. I thought it was that other fella."

"What other fella?"

"The one that owns that office."

"Do you know who he is?"

"Yeah, he's the manager."

"The manager of what?"

"He's the manager of the football team."

"*No, he's not!* He's the manager of this building."

"Well, someone tol' me he was the manager of the football team."

Police Sgt. Walt Franklin came running up the stairs with two other officers.

"*Hey, Wesson!* What's going on? Someone called and said there was an explosion in the HUB."

"Well, it wasn't a bomb. It was a shotgun fired by, *guess who?*"

The Sergeant looked at the damaged ceiling, the shotgun, and then Richard.

"*Oh, my God!* What happened?"

"Danny will explain it all. He'll have to write up the arrest report and transport Richard to the King County jail."

"Why *me?*" protested Danny.

"You're in charge, remember? I only assist you until I'm off this other assignment."

Danny started laughing.

"What's so funny?" asked Wesson.

"Now they can call us 'Smith and Wesson,'" referring to a gun manufacturer.

Wesson laughed and shook his head. "Don't forget to read him his rights, Danny."

He checked the office to make sure he wasn't leaving anything behind, and then went back into the hall, closing and locking the door behind him. Some of the students were milling around and one asked what had happened.

"You know that guy who's been hanging around here, the one with the baseball cap with a "W" on it?"

"Ya mean that old guy? What'd he do?"

"He tried to kill me for one thing."

"Jeez!"

"He won't be around for a while, but if you ever see him again, give me a call," he said as he passed out a few business cards.

Then he walked over to the police office to check his mail and phone messages. When he entered the door, he could hear Richard in one of the back rooms yelling and swearing as they strip searched him before taking him to jail.

Wesson didn't have any mail, but he went into his office and checked for phone messages. There was only one, but it was a hang up. He left his office locking the door behind him. It was now five o'clock and he decided to call it a day and go home.

Wesson and his wife of six months, Jenny, had a wonderful fourteenth floor apartment overlooking Puget Sound in the town of Edmonds, just a few miles north of Seattle. He had even set up a telescope on his deck to see the names of ships in the daylight hours and to explore the heavens during the night. It was a great place for him and his bride.

As soon as he came through the door, Jenny was waiting for him. She hugged and kissed him, and was so happy to see him.

"Let's go out for dinner tonight, George."

"Sounds good to me."

They lived within walking distance of six restaurants, and settled on an Italian bistro. As they enjoyed their dinner and wine, Jenny smiled at him.

"So why did you have to work on a Saturday," she asked.

"Have you been watching the news at all on TV?" asked Wesson.

"No. Why?"

"Well, I was on a news conference."

"Really? Oh I wish I had known. Maybe it'll be on the eleven o'clock news tonight."

"Maybe. So what have you been doing?"

"You know that job opening at the bookstore?"

"Yeah."

"Well they called me today to tell me I have it. They want me to come in Monday."

"Hey, that's great."

"I'm so thrilled about it."

"I think it's wonderful."

"It would have been a perfect day if it weren't for the other phone calls."

"Oh? What other calls?"

"I don't know. They were kind of weird."

"What do you mean?"

"Well, the phone would ring, and I'm sure someone was there, but they wouldn't say anything."

"Sometimes we get these computer calls, and all we hear is a click. Was it like that?"

"No. I could hear background noise, and I think I could hear someone breathing."

"Was there only one call?"

"No. Maybe four."

"They were all the same? You could hear someone, but he wouldn't say anything?"

"Yeah."

Wesson suddenly became silent. They finished their meal and began their walk back home. It was a beautiful evening. It had rained in the afternoon, but now the skies were clear and the stars looked as if they extended down to the waters of Puget Sound. It was such a romantic sight. But, Wesson didn't feel romantic.

"Jenny, I want you to go home to your parents for a while."

She was stunned.

"What? Why?"

"I can't tell you."

She began to cry.

"George, it was such a beautiful evening, and now you don't want me around? Why? Is there someone *else?*"

"Jenny, I love you with all my heart, but if you don't leave, you'll be in deadly danger."

"Does this have something to do with those phone calls?"

"Yes."

"Were those calls for you?"

"Yes, I think so."

"George, what's going on?"

"Jenny, the more you know, the greater the risk."

"This means I won't get the job."

"I know, and I feel terrible about it. You'll have other opportunities."

"Will Spokane be far enough away?"

"I hope so. Come on let's get you packed. I want you on the earliest shuttle flight we can make."

"George, if I find out you're just trying to get rid of me, I'm gonna *kill* you."

Chapter 12
The Day of the Gun

George and Jenny parked their Honda CRV in the SeaTac airport parking lot in time to catch the nine o'clock morning shuttle flight to Spokane. After purchasing Jenny's ticket, they walked up to the security screeners on the way to the boarding gate.

"I'm a police officer and I'm carrying a weapon," Wesson said to one of the inspectors.

"Just a minute, sir," said the black female.

She walked up to a man in white shirt sleeves and tie. Wesson could see her talking with the man and pointing at him. The man nodded and walked toward him.

"Hi," said the man. Are you carrying a gun?"

Wesson spread his coat open so the man could see the holstered Glock.

"Would you come with me into this office?" said the man as he pointed to a door. Wesson took a quick look for Jenny and saw her sitting on a chair. They both made a little wave at each other.

"Who's that?" asked the man.

"It's my wife."

The man opened the door and Wesson could see a table and a couple chairs.

"Have a seat."

They both sat at the table facing each other.

"Please give me your gun," said the man calmly and professionally.

"Before I do, what will you do with it?" responded George nervously.

"If you're who you say you are we'll take care of it for you," said the man trying to placate the detective.

Wesson was the kind of guy that liked to argue and resist, but he decided this was not the place. He slowly took the gun out of its holster with his right hand. He then took hold of the end of the barrel with his left hand and gave it to the man, butt first.

The man took the gun and removed the magazine from its grip. He then pulled back the slide and ejected the round that was chambered, which fell onto the table.

"OK," said the man firmly, "now let's see some ID."

Wesson produced all of the required pieces of paper and his shield, satisfying National Security agent that he was not a threat.

"Okay, you can continue to the departure gate," said the agent.

"What are you going to do with my gun?"

"We'll give it back to you outside on the sidewalk, when you're ready to leave."

Wesson nodded and then left the room and met up with his wife.

"We gotta go through this every time," complained Jenny.

Wesson just smiled at her as they walked to the gate.

"You don't have to see me off, George."

"Oh, I don't mind." he responded.

When they reached the gate, they sat down next to each other, waiting for the boarding announcement. They had about fifteen minutes together.

"George, are you going to tell me why I have to leave."

"I'd like to Jenny, but I can't. If you stayed here, I would worry about you all of the time, and then I wouldn't be effective.

"Is someone after you?"

Wesson paused and thought before he answered.

"I'm not sure, Jen. There might be. It's just that I have a bad feeling."

"Oh, George. You should leave too."

"Jen, someone's life may be on the line. I can't leave him."

An announcement came over the speaker for passengers to start boarding.

"Whatever you do, Jenny, don't tell anyone the real reason for your trip."

"They're going to ask where you are. What should I say?"

"That's up to you. Tell them we had a fight, or anything else you can think of. Just don't say anything about the calls or what I've just told you. I mean it."

Jenny got in line with the boarding passengers.

"George, I'll pray for you."

Wesson gave her a small wave as she went down the boarding ramp. He stayed at the gate until he could see her plane lift off the runway.

On the drive back to Seattle, he felt relieved to have his wife out of harm's way. The next thing he planned to do was to change his telephone number and have it unlisted.

He arrived at his apartment around ten o'clock, and as soon as he entered, he could see the light on his phone indicating there was a message. He picked up the handset and heard his voicemail recorded operator announce:

"You have three unheard messages. The first message was left this morning at eight thirty." Click. There was some background noises and then, click, the caller hung up.

"To save this message press nine, to delete press seven."

He deleted the message.

"Next message, left this morning at nine fifteen."

"Hello, George."

It was Hunter's voice.

"I've been getting several hang-up calls on my voice mail, and I was wondering if you were trying to get a hold of me. I'll be home most of the day and evening if you want to try again."

Wesson saved this message.

"Next message left this morning at nine thirty-three." Click.

"End of messages."

He hung up the phone, sank into a chair, and waited for the phone to ring. He knew it would soon, and he didn't have to wait long.

Ring-g-g-g.

"Hello?"

There was no response, but he could hear ambient noise like a phone was off the hook.

"*Hello?!*"

Still no answer.

Then he heard the rattle of the door knob. He turned just in time to see it rotate about an inch.

He dropped the phone, un-holstered his Glock, and ran to the door. His heart was beating fast, and he could feel it pounding against his ribs. He couldn't bring himself to open the door. He was sweating profusely and shaking badly.

Open the door! Open the door! he kept telling himself. Finally he got up the courage to unlock the door, turn the knob and pull it open. He pushed the gun in front of him as he moved out into the hall. He heard the elevator stop down the hall and its door slide open. He ran to it keeping his gun in front of him. Two women and a man in the elevator were suddenly confronted by Wesson, who to them was a wild looking man with a gun. The women screamed, and the man quickly punched the close door button. The door closed and they disappeared. Wesson continued moving to the end of the hall where there was a window. He looked out on to the street below and saw a man in white coveralls walking from the street entrance of the building to a white van. He got in and drove away.

Wesson stood helplessly looking down on the street when he heard approaching sirens. Two City of Edmond's patrol cars stopped next to the building. Two officers got out from each car and approached the entrance.

He holstered his gun and went back to his apartment. He left the door ajar and sat down in his TV chair and waited. It didn't take long.

There was a rap on his door.

"Police. Can we come in?"

"It's open."

A big burly cop pushed the door open, and stepped into the room with another officer behind him. The other two officers stayed out in the hall.

"Can I have your name please?"

"George Wesson."

"Mr. Wesson, do you own a gun?"

"Yes," said Wesson as he slouched in the chair.

"May I see it?"

Without a word, George opened his coat. The officer went up to him and pulled the Glock out of its holster. He examined it and pulled the slide back to confirm it was loaded.

"This looks like a police weapon, what are you doing with it?"

"I'm a police officer."

"Really? What department."

"The University of Washington."

"Can you prove it?"

Wesson reached into his coat pocket.

"Here's my shield, my ID, and my permit for the gun."

"I believe you," said the officer as he returned the gun. "But, I think you still got some explaining to do."

"OK, shoot. I mean, ask away."

"Well, for starters, you just about caused three people to have heart failure,"

"Yeah, I know, I feel really sorry about that."

"How did that happen?"

"I was chasing someone down the hall and the elevator opened. They saw me with a gun and they got scared."

"Who were you chasing?"

This caused Wesson to be wary. Hunter had warned him about telling anyone about AM

"I'm not sure."

"Did you see someone?"

"By the time I got out into the hallway, he was gone. Look, officer, believe me there was a rational reason for what I did. I don't think it'll happen again. I'll personally apologize to those people on the elevator."

"Why don't you do that now? They're waiting on the next floor down in the game room."

Wesson followed them down the hall to the stairs. He kept thinking how he must have overreacted, and wished he hadn't panicked. He felt so unprofessional.

They went down the stairs one level, down the hall and into the game room. The two women and the man Wesson frightened were there.

"Well, I see you caught him," said the man.

"Turns out this man is a cop," said the police officer.

"Look," said Wesson, "I'm really sorry I startled you. Someone was trying to get into my room and I chased him down the hall and...."

Wesson suddenly caught sight of a telephone on a table in a back corner of the room. He walked over to it and saw the handset had not been hung up, but was just lying on the table. He put the receiver to his ear and realized it was an open line.

He turned to the people standing there.

"Have you seen anyone use this phone?"

They looked at him and shrugged.

"Is this the phone you used to call the police?"

"No," said the man. "I used the phone on this table here. I didn't even notice that one."

"And you didn't notice anyone else use it."

"Not since we've been here."

Wesson quickly ran out of the room and up the stairs and then into his room. He picked up his phone off of the floor and put it to his ear. He could still hear them talking in the game room.

"Are you sure that guy's a cop."

"I believe he is."

"I think he's wacko. Look here. He didn't even hang up the phone."

Click.

Chapter 13
A Strange Case

On Monday morning, Wesson went to the Behavioral Sciences Building and sat down in his office. He wanted to talk with Professor Hunter, but he hadn't shown up yet. After he checked his email, there wasn't much to do, so he idled away his time by playing computer games.

Finally, Hunter came into the outer office.

"George, was that you trying to call me this weekend?"

"No. I didn't call you. This guy, AM, do you think he'd fool around by calling and trying to unnerve you?"

"I don't know."

"Well, someone got to me yesterday."

Hunter looked concerned.

"What happened?"

Wesson told Hunter about fearing for his wife's safety and sending her to her parents, the phone calls, someone trying to get into his condo and his run in with the Edmonds' police. "George, give me a few minutes and then come into my office. Let's talk about it."

"Fine."

Wesson's phone rang. He was hesitant to even answer it, but Hunter was standing nearby waiting to see if AM was calling. He picked up the hand set.

"Lt. Wesson."

"Hey, George. It's Danny."

"Hi Danny. What's going on"

"Could you come over to the Communications Building? We've got something weird going on here."

"Sure. Where are you in the building?"

"Second floor hallway in front of the women's restroom."

"I'll be right over."

Then he hung up.

"Michael, something's come up. I'll meet with you a little later."

"Okay."

The Communications Building was just next door, so it only took a couple of minutes for him to get there. He climbed the stairs to the second floor, where he saw Danny with two uniformed cops talking to a woman.

"What's going on, Danny?"

"George, this is Susan Meadian. She's an instructor in this building. I'll let her tell the story."

Wesson turned to her. She was a petite dark complexioned woman about 30 years old. Maybe Hispanic.

"I went into this restroom," she began, "and sat down in a stall. Then I saw a metal object come up from under the panel separating the stall next door."

"What did you do?" asked Wesson.

"It scared me to death. So, I ran out into the hall, and I used my cell phone to call the police."

"Did anyone besides you come out?"

"No. I've been here the whole time, but no one else came out."

One of the uniformed officers pushed open the door and called out, "Hello. Anyone in here?"

No one answered.

"Come on out or we're coming *in*!"

A falsetto voice responded. "I'm having a difficult period."

The officers looked at each other and shrugged.

"We'll give you three minutes. If you're not out by then, we're coming in."

They heard a toilet flush, and then someone moving around. Footsteps approached the door from the inside of the restroom. Then the door opened. Standing before the gaping officers was a tall figure in a dress, high heels and a hat, and looking very frightened.

"Can I please have your name?" asked Wesson as he approached.

"Uh, Roger," said the person in a male voice.

"Are you a *man?*"

"Yes."

"What were you doing in there?"

"I was just sitting there."

"Danny, take a look and see if he left anything."

Wesson continued to question Roger as Danny went into the restroom.

"What are you doing on campus?"

"I'm a PhD candidate in Political Science."

Danny came back out of the restroom with a small backpack.

"I found this."

"Is this your bag?"

"No."

"Then you won't mind if I open it."

"Yes, I do mind."

"I thought you said it wasn't yours?"

"It is mine."

"Okay," said Wesson. "The fact you won't let us open your bag means you must have something to hide. So we'll get a search warrant. We'll also include your house and car."

"You're treating me like a *criminal*. I haven't done anything wrong."

"How come you're dressed in women's clothes?"

"Because I like to. It's not a crime, is it?"

"If you're a man, why were you in the women's restroom?"

"Dressed like this, I couldn't go into the men's restroom."

"I see your point," said Wesson. "But, when you entered the women's restroom, you stepped over the line of lewd behavior, or voyeurism and that is a crime."

Roger was shaking, and looked away from Wesson.

"Where do you live, Roger?"

"Married student housing, off campus."

"You're *married?*"

Tears formed in his eyes.

"Yes."

"Does your wife know about your behavior?"

"No."

"Well, unfortunately she's going to find out when we search your apartment."

"Go ahead! Open the bag!"

Danny rifled through the bag and found Roger's regular clothes, and a telescoping metal tube.

"It was the end of that tube I saw sticking into my stall," said Susan Meadian.

"This is a toy periscope," said Wesson as he examined it. "Danny, read him his rights and cuff him."

"What are you going to do?" cried Roger.

"We're going to arrest you and take you to jail," said Danny.

"You can't take me like *this*! Let me change clothes! What will they do to *me*?!"

The uniformed officers started laughing.

"They'll be glad to see you," said one of the officers.

"*Nooooo! Nooooo! Please!*" he begged.

Wesson was afraid Roger was going to have a stroke.

"Listen, Roger," said Wesson. "You go with the officers to the police office, and you can change your clothes there. Danny's going to fill out some paperwork on you then take you to the county jail."

Roger kept wailing as he was led down the stairs, out the door, and placed into a patrol car.

Wesson and Susan Meadian were the only ones left standing in the hall.

"I'm sorry all this had to happen."

"The poor man," said Susan. "Do you think he'll be alright?"

"I don't know. He must be some kind of transvestite. I just hope no one hurts him in jail."

"It's sad," she said as they walked down the stairs and out the door. "Is there some way I can check up on him?"

"I suppose by calling the county jail."

"Okay," she said smiling. "Thanks."

"Bye," said Wesson.

Wesson stood there for a moment, shook his head, saying to himself, "What next?" then walked back over to his office in the Behavioral Sciences Building.

Chapter 14
Bait

Wesson entered the outer office of the Sociology Department and saw that Dr. Hunter's door was open. He poked his head into the professor's office.

"I'm back, Michael."

"Where did you go?"

"There was a little problem in the Communications Building, and my partner wanted me to come over to help him."

"Was it something serious?"

"Not really."

"It's about lunch time," said Hunter. "Let's get a bite to eat while we talk."

"Sounds good. Where would you like to go?"

"Let's go to the HUB."

"Okay."

The weather was cool and clear as they walked on the path to the HUB. The trees were turning into bright colors and losing their leaves. The days of frost were not too far away.

They entered the HUB through the main doors of the building and went down a flight of stairs to the cafeteria. After buying sandwiches and coffee, they found all of the tables were taken except for some near the back of the room, where a black student was sitting at one.

Wesson and Hunter set their trays down at an empty table and settled into their chairs.

"You can't sit there," said the young man.

Wesson looked at him.

"No? Why not?"

"Because that table's reserved."

"By whom?"

"By the Organization of Black Students."

"Never heard of them."

"When my friends show up, you're gonna get your butt kicked," said the young man, who then walked away.

"I wonder how long this has been going on?" said Wesson aloud.

"What's he doing?" asked Hunter.

"The cafeteria gets full during lunch and some of these black guys save these tables for their friends."

"I think you're going to get an argument. He's coming back with some of those friends," said the professor.

A large muscular black man walked up to Wesson.

"I'm Jeffery Taylor an' you're sittin' in ma chair."

"I'm sorry, Jeffery, but I didn't see your name on it anywhere."

Jeffery swept a hand indicating three empty tables even though all other tables were filled.

"These are our tables an' we don't want no whiteys."

"Don't want no…? Are you really a student here?"

Wesson touched a nerve.

"Yes, I'm a student! I'm on the football team!" said Jeffery indignantly.

"I would never admit I was on the team, the way they're playing," said Wesson. "I wouldn't want to play with a bunch of losers."

"You git outta ma chair, or I'll whup your ass!" said the angry young man.

Wesson stood up with his eyes locked on to Jeffery's, and pulled out his police shield.

"You try to whup my ass, and I'll shoot your ass."

A defeated Jeffery had the wind knocked out of his sails.

"You're a cop?"

"You and your friends are welcome to sit with us if you want. But you are not going to intimidate others and keep them from sitting at these tables. Discrimination works both ways, and if we get complaints we will arrest you or anyone else. I'll bet your parents are proud of you. How would they like to see your picture in the paper for something other than football?"

Jeffery and his entourage decide to leave and find another place to have lunch. Wesson sat down, smiled, and looked at Hunter who was surprised by the encounter.

"I guess they weren't hungry after all," said Wesson.

Just then, James Wilson, the HUB manager, walked up.

"Thank you, Lt. Wesson. I was about to call you about this problem."

"If it happens again, let me know, Jim."

"How did things turn out on Saturday?"

"You won't see Richard for a while. He'll either be in jail or at the funny farm."

"What happened?"

"He was coming after you with a shotgun."

"No kidding? Did you shoot him?"

"No. But, he nearly shot me."

"I don't know what to say. Thank you."

"No problem."

After the manager left, Dr. Hunter was shaking his head.

"You lead a pretty active life, don't you?"

"I seem to keep busy."

"Are you ever bothered by the stress of the job?"

"That's what I want to talk about, Michael. The day to day kinds of things really don't bother me because I feel I can handle them. In my mind, I can see what I have to do, and I just do it. It also helps to carry the authority of a badge and a gun. But, this AM thing does bother me. I don't understand it. I'm becoming almost paranoid, thinking he's out to get me. He probably doesn't even know who I am, or that I've even been assigned to find him."

Hunter cleared his throat and avoided looking at Wesson's face.

"He knows who you are, George."

"What do you mean?"

"You told him who you were."

"When?"

"At the news conference."

"Wait a minute! You guys set me up. Didn't you?"

"It wasn't my idea."

"*Whose*, then?"

"Your boss."

"You mean the Chief?"

"Yes."

"Who else is involved?"

"Denney and me. You see, George, we knew it would be impossible for us to find AM, so we decided to have him come to us."

"I see. So, you're using me as bait."

"What I'm really surprised at," said Hunter, "is that he'd make contact with you so soon."

"That's all you've got to say? You not only put *me* in jeopardy, but also my *wife!*"

Wesson was furious. How could his friend and teacher be so callous as to not even warn him? Hunter's face was red from embarrassment.

"I'm sorry, George. I truly wish we hadn't done this. But, we can't back up."

Wesson could feel his cheeks burning as he sat across from Hunter. He had a lot of reasons to be angry, but he then thought, now it was better that he take the time to learn more about his predicament than complain. He put his hand in his coat pocket and turned on the recorder.

"You've heard from him haven't you?"

"Yes."

"What did he want?"

"He wanted credit for my study of criminal types."

"Should he have credit?"

"No. The only thing he did was to find the inmates whose identification number I'd give to the prison guard. I wanted to use AM to impress upon the inmates the need for truthful answers to my questions. I would have expected them to give phony information to screw up the data. But, AM was supposed to tell them to be straight with me."

"Did he do that? Did he threaten them?"

"I don't know. The answers the inmates gave to my questions seemed reasonable."

"So, you tried to stiff him, and leave without giving him anything."

"He said he wanted freedom. I couldn't give him that."

"Then he tricked you with a planned riot, chopped off your hand, and took off."

"Yes."

"How did he know you'd published the study?"

"He's not dumb. He must have bought a textbook, or has seen one of the papers I've written."

"You know what I think, Michael? I don't think he's alone. He's been getting help from one or more other people."

"That might be. It would explain how he seems to be in two places at the same time."

Wesson thought more about why he found himself in a bad dream. It wouldn't have worked to have the city police get involved, because they wouldn't put enough time or effort into the case. Besides, the UW didn't want it known there was a maniac running loose on the campus. He had often argued with the Chief that the campus police force should be able to handle its own business without calling in outsiders. So, who else was going to do it? He was the only detective on the case. Danny had to take care of all of the day to day problems of stolen bicycles or lunches, so he could put in full effort. It was logical he was the only one.

Wesson and Hunter returned to their offices. The professor worked on his lesson plans, and the detective sat at his computer trying to think what to do.

What are the main traits of a Sociopath? he thought.

He really wasn't sure. He kind of knew, because of Hunter's writings and lectures. He decided to look up the subject on the internet and did a Google search on his computer. There was a lot of information. He looked at some of the major traits to see if he could imagine such a person.

Paranoia. Hmmm, he thought to himself. *I wonder if that's more likely a trait of the victim. I'm becoming paranoid.*

He tries to control every aspect of the victim.

He's incapable of feeing remorse or guilt.

He exhibits extreme narcissism.

The rest of the traits were really that of a crazy person. What bothered Wesson was, maybe AM was not crazy. Granted, he wasn't normal, but he seems too smart. It gave him a cold chill to think this sociopath may be smarter than anyone looking for him.

He was suddenly startled by his telephone ringing. He paused before answering. *Maybe it's him,* he thought. He hoped it was. If he could talk to him, maybe it would get rid of some of the apprehension he felt.

After it rang for the third time, he lifted the receiver from the cradle.

"George Wesson," he spoke.

"George? It's Paul Gillette."

It was Captain Gillette, the day shift patrol commander.

"Hi, Paul. What can I do for you?" he asked, sensing this wasn't a social call.

"I need your help for a few hours tomorrow."

"What's going on?"

"We have a guest speaker coming on campus, and we need some help with crowd control. Come into the office at eight o'clock tomorrow morning for a planning meeting."

"What kind of guest speaker?"

Gillette paused a moment and then said, "He's the head of the American Nazi Party."

Chapter 15
The Nazi

The next morning, Wesson arrived at the University Police office just in time to attend the eight o'clock briefing. It wasn't too unusual to have famous or controversial people visit and give lectures, but this was a first to have someone from the Nazi Party.

A thought came to the detective's mind. *Could there possibly be a connection between the murder and the arrival of such a maligned person on campus?*

He couldn't shake the idea, even though it's more likely to just be a coincidence. So, he welcomed the diversion in that he may pick up an idea or a clue; besides, he wanted to see and hear this Nazi.

The briefing was held in the lunchroom. Looking around, George could see about ten uniformed officers. He and Danny were the only ones in street clothes. Captain Gillette stood up and the room became quite.

"OK, here's what we got. Grant Lincoln, the head of the American Nazi Party, will be on campus for one hour, beginning at ten o'clock this morning. He's going to give a forty-five minute lecture at Meany Auditorium, followed by fifteen minutes of questions and answers. Our job is to escort him to and from the building and to make sure he doesn't get killed somewhere in between. I'll select some of you to escort him to and from the rear access to the building, and the rest of you will work crowd control at the main entrance."

"What about Danny and me?" asked George.

"You guys will be inside the building. In your civvies, you'll blend in with the attendees."

"You mean just the *two* of us are going to protect this guy from mob violence if things get out of hand?"

"Just keep on your toes. There'll be some of us up on the stage with him if something should happen."

"I dunno, Paul. I don't think you've got enough people to protect him. Ya know there're probably a lot of Jewish students that lost family and relatives to the Nazis. They might want to tear this guy to shreds."

"Well, these are all of the people I could come up with."

"What are we supposed to do if the students decide to rush the stage?"

"Look, George, there are two main aisles. You and Danny sit up near the front, each of you next to an aisle. If the crowd rushes the stage, all you have to do is step into the aisle and slow them down. That'll give us time to get Lincoln off of the stage, through the back door and into a car."

"What about *us*!' cried, Danny?

Gillette thought a moment, and then smiled.

"You're pretty hefty guys. I think you can take a little pushing and shoving."

The meeting broke up and they had a little over an hour before they had to be at the auditorium.

"C'mon, Danny, let's go to the HUB and I'll buy you a cup of Starbucks instead of lunchroom coffee."

The HUB was close to the Meany Auditorium, so it was a good place to hang out. They took one of the police cruisers and parked in the lot next to the building, went in, got a scone and coffee then sat down at one of the tables.

"George, you're kind of quiet. What are you thinking?"

"I'm just wondering if there's a connection to the killing and this Nazi guy."

"Really? What could that be?"

"I dunno. It just seems weird to me that he shows up right after this thing happens."

"You think the girl was Jewish, and he's trying to make a statement?"

"Naw, she wasn't Jewish. I think she was a random victim. But, maybe he knows who killed her. Maybe he's in on it and is using the murder to somehow further his cause."

"What is his cause?"

"To stir people up. To get attention."

"Huh! Maybe you're on to something, George."

"The Nazi Party has probably got lots of money. Maybe they're supporting this madman AM guy to commit some heinous crime, and then when everyone is excited about that, they come in and play on people's emotions."

"Wow, George! Have you told anyone else what you think?"

"No, just you, Danny. I just thought it up. Anyway," he said, draining his cup of coffee, "I think it's time to head over to the auditorium. We'll want to stake out our seats before people start showing up."

They walked across the street to Meany Hall and saw a couple of uniformed officers who were screening the early arrivals. Another officer at the door recognized them and let them in. The large auditorium was empty now, but soon it would fill with students, clamoring to get their hands on the famous hatemonger. Wesson didn't like having such a character spewing his venom, but the University policy makers felt it was important to have an open forum for all points of view. So, it was his job to help keep this scum out of the clutches of an enraged audience.

The doors were opened and the students began to file in. Wesson and Danny chose their seats and waited for the auditorium to fill. After only waiting for about five minutes, the house lights were dimmed and the entrance doors were closed. The stage lights were turned up and a very nervous young woman came out from behind the curtain, followed by Grant Lincoln, wearing a long overcoat and was flanked by two police officers.

"Good morning," she said. "I'm Beth Hanson from the Special Events Office, and I want to welcome you to this morning's presentation by…."

She couldn't finish the announcement as the building shook with cat calls, oaths and boos. She hurriedly left the stage, and then Lincoln strode up to the microphone. He was a tall slim man about 35 with Aryan features, blond hair and blue eyes.

Suddenly, he threw off his overcoat. He was dressed like a storm trooper from the days of Hitler. He wore a red armband with a swastika inside a white circle. He placed his hands on his hips and turned his body a little to the left so the swastika on his right arm could clearly be seen by everyone. He stood there without saying a word and just stared back at the audience.

Chapter 16
The Maddened Crowd

As Grant Lincoln, the Nazi, stood before his raucous audience, he exuded self-confidence. Wesson was reminded of old film clips of Hitler standing silently before crowds without uttering a word. Now, this Nazi was doing the same.

The effect was almost immediate. It was like oil poured onto a stormy sea. The noise abated until it was completely quiet, and still he stood there without saying a word, with an arrogant grin on his face.

Wesson was beginning to think that it was all a sham and the Nazi wasn't going to speak at all, but then he heard an almost inaudible voice. It was low and guttural, yet easily understood, even through the twisted evil grin.

"I want to thank President Denney and all who were responsible for allowing me to speak at your great university."

His grin now faded into an amicable smile. He was now speaking at a normal volume.

"I especially want to thank the University Police and Chief Meyer for providing protection for me while I am here. " Then he added with a chuckle, "However, I've always been able to take care of myself."

He now began to pace back and forth across the stage as if he were searching for his next words. Then he stopped and again faced the audience.

"You know, we are a small party. We can't afford to put on extravagant dinners or advertising to bring in money to support our cause. But, we manage to get attention without paying for it."

He went quiet for a moment to let that statement soak in.

"It works, doesn't it? I mean, you've all heard of us. Do you know, how?"

He paused again to let his words take hold.

"You've heard about us through the news media. That's right, the news media."

Wesson could hear murmurs going through the crowd of listeners.

"Everywhere I go," continued Lincoln, "the news media goes! Why? It's because, I cause exciting things to happen."

Wesson looked around and sure enough he could see at least two television cameras at the rear of the auditorium.

"I make inflammatory remarks that stir up the crowds, and I will do the same here and now!"

Then he clicked his heels and threw out his right arm in a Nazi salute and shouted, "*Heil!*"

As he predicted, the crowded auditorium went wild. People leapt from their seats in a chorus that was impossible for Wesson to distinguish the words being shouted.

Lincoln drew his lips back into a sneer as he shouted back a diatribe of racial slurs. He made a statement that blacks would be happier in Africa, and all of America's traitors have been Jewish.

Then above the din, a young woman's voice could be heard.

"Your people killed my grandmother in Auschwitz!"

All heard the voice and briefly quieted.

Lincoln mocked her by pointing and then shouting, "Your grandmother was a Jew and deserved to die!"

The volume of human voices reached a new level. Then another voice was heard.

"Did you murder that girl?"

There was another lull.

"You mean that one on campus? She got what she deserved."

Wesson wondered if the Nazi was really admitting to the crime, or was he just using it to antagonize the crowd even more? The effect of the statement was immediate and beyond its intended purpose.

Now Wesson could feel the whole building begin to shake. He saw the officers standing next to the Nazi suddenly tense and their eyes widen. Turning around he could see a human avalanche spilling down the aisles and over the seatbacks. He quickly did his job and stepped out into the aisle. He was suddenly hit in the back like a single ten pin being struck by a fusillade of bowling balls. He was slammed to the floor and trampled on like a mat. He rolled over on his side and tried to protect his groin. One foot dug into his ribs and dislodged his pistol that was now being stepped on. Using every ounce of energy he had left, he squirmed toward it, reached out his hand and grasped it.

Then it was over. The auditorium was almost empty. A news reporter who had been standing near the back of the auditorium came running down the aisle and helped Wesson to his feet. Looking over to where he last saw Danny, Wesson could see some movement.

"Danny, are you alright?"

"I think so. Man, what happened?"

"I think it was a stampede," said the detective as he re-holstered his gun.

"What happened to the Nazi?" asked Danny.

"I don't really care."

"George, you look terrible," said Danny. "You got a couple of pretty good shiners."

"Yeah, they drove my face into the floor and then stepped on my head."

"Maybe you should go to the infirmary."

Wesson's vision was narrowing down to just a couple of slits. He brushed off his sport coat, and then shrugged.

"I'll make it OK. Let's walk over to the office. I've got a couple of things to say to Gillette."

When they reached the office, the other officers who were on the detail were returning. All of them were hyped up about the big commotion the Nazi caused.

"Man, did ya see those kids comin' right over the seatbacks?" said one laughing. "It looked like a tsunami."

"The stupid jerk never got to his point," said another. "I don't think anyone knows what he was gonna say."

"Hello, George," said Captain Gillette. "Boy, you and Danny look like you've been through a war."

"Yeah, I want to talk to you about that."

"You guys did a great job," said the Captain. "You slowed them down just enough so we could get the guy out the back door and into a car."

"You mean he got away OK."

"Yeah, some of them caught his arm for just an instant, but we pulled him away and saved his bacon."

"Gee, that's too bad," said Wesson. "I was hoping they'd make hamburger out of him."

"Sorry, you guys got roughed up. I'll drive you over to the infirmary to get checked out."

Both were reluctant, but knew they had to go as it was policy for injuries on the job.

"One more thing, Captain, I think we should get combat pay," said Danny.

"And, the Purple Heart," added Wesson.

Chapter 17
Anxiety

It was one o'clock in the afternoon by the time the detective was finished at the infirmary. He returned to the police office to pick up his car, and drove to the Behavioral Sciences Building.

As soon as he walked through the door of the Sociology Department, he was met by Professor Hunter, who was standing by his secretary's desk.

"George, what happened to you? Did you get hit by a car or something?"

"It feels like it."

"Wow, you're all bandaged up and you got two black eyes. You can't tell me you walked into a door."

"Did you hear about the Nazi who was on campus?"

"I heard something about it. Did he do this to you?"

"Naw, it was his fan club. But, I've got a new theory, Michael."

"About what?" asked the professor as he started walking back to his office, with Wesson in tow.

"Well, maybe there's a connection with the murder and the Nazi being in town."

"Oh, come on, George. Where did you get an idea like that?" said Hunter as he sat down at his desk.

"Maybe he's trying to make a statement, or cause a big commotion. He even said he gets free press by stirring people up."

Professor Hunter wasn't buying the detective's theory. He sat upright and shook his head.

"No, George. Our killer likes to work alone."

Wesson felt deflated, but he wasn't going to give up on his idea. He would wait until he had proof before bringing the subject up again.

After their conversation ended, Wesson made his way back to his desk, and decided to do some research with information he did have about the killer. Time flew by and before he realized it, evening had come.

At seven o'clock, he shut down his computer and got ready to leave for the day. Hunter was teaching an evening class, and nearly all of the staff members were gone. He felt a chill in the air as he walked to his car. The days were getting noticeably shorter and in a few more weeks, it would be dark by five o'clock.

He started out on his usual route home. After he got onto the freeway, he noticed the headlights of a car that seemed to be pacing him.

Could someone really be following me? he thought.

He slowed down, hoping the following car would go around him. The car behind him slowed too, still staying with him. This really unnerved him. He quickly changed lanes and tromped on the accelerator. The car behind him did exactly the same, keeping right on his tail. Now Wesson changed back to the outside lane and suddenly slowed down. The other car did the same maneuver with great skill, and then began to advance on him. Wesson took his gun out of the holster and placed it on the seat beside him.

The other car was almost on his rear bumper, when suddenly everything erupted in a bright flash of lights; red and blue flashing lights.

The very first thought that came to Wesson was to run. The second thought was to pick up the gun and shoot himself. He didn't do either and pulled onto the shoulder and stopped.

He sat there for what seemed like eternity with a bright spotlight shining through the rear window of his car. He thought about hiding the gun but knew if the state trooper would see him do it, he'd really be in trouble. So, he just sat there and waited while trooper ran his license plate on his computer

Finally, Wesson could see the officer approach in his side mirror. He rolled down his window and was greeted by a flashlight beam in his eyes. The first words uttered by the trooper were, "Please step out of the car."

The trooper was shocked to see Wesson condition with bandages and two black eyes.

"What the hell happened to you?" he said. "It looks like you've already been in an accident."

"Oh, well I was at this lecture given by a Nazi when…."

He knew he had already said too much, as the officer just gaped at him.

Wesson obeyed every command he was given. He was patted down and then told to stand in back of his car.

"Will you give me permission to search your vehicle?" asked the trooper.

"Yes."

"Before I do, will I find any surprises?"

"I don't think so."

"You don't have any other weapons other than the Glock I see on the passenger seat?"

"No."

The trooper searched the car thoroughly and was satisfied there were no other weapons or illegal drugs.

"Now, I want to see your permit for the gun."

Wesson fished it out of his wallet and gave it to him.

The officer held the flashlight under his arm while he unfolded and examined the document

"You're a police officer?" asked the trooper with surprise.

"Yeah," said Wesson as he dug out his shield and identification.

"Do you know why I pulled you over?"

"I can guess."

"What were you doing? First you'd slow down, then speed up and change lanes, slow down, change lanes again. You looked like you were trying to ditch me."

This was very difficult for Wesson. It seems like he's made himself look foolish to every other police jurisdiction in the area.

"I'm highly embarrassed. I know how this must look to you, Officer, but there was a rational reason for what I did. But, I can't tell you about it."

"Why not?"

"Because you might think I'm crazy."

"I already think you're nuts. I'm trying to decide whether to arrest you, or give you a $500 ticket."

"Listen, I can assure you I'm not drunk, and I've never tried drugs. If you think you've got to give me a ticket, go ahead."

The trooper looked over Wesson's identification.

"You stand right here. I'm going to run the rest of this information on the computer" he said as he returned to his car and punched in the data.

There is an on-line data base that has every North American police officer's profile and status. This will prove whether or not Wesson is for real.

The trooper returned holding a computer printout which included photos of Wesson's face, and a handwriting sample.

"You're lucky. I'm just going to give you an expensive ticket."

"Thanks. I guess."

"You know, I've been thinking. You probably thought someone was stalking you, and you were trying to get away."

Wesson didn't say anything, and he was now wondering if the trooper was real or not. But, he must be. He had a computer in his car, the uniform, the nameplate, the equipment . . . .

"Does this have anything to do with your job?"

"Yes. It does."

"You want to tell me about it?" asked the trooper with concern.

"I *can't* tell you about it. It's almost like dealing with a disease. If I did tell you, you might become infected, too."

"Man, that's weird! Maybe you should see a doc."

"Look. Just write the ticket. I want to go home."

"Forget the ticket. Go on home. Get some help, will ya?"

Wesson thanked the trooper, returned to his car and continued the drive home. He could see the trooper following, and then turn off after a couple of miles.

It was after eight o'clock when he reached his condo. He was still shaken from his experience, but glad he wasn't arrested or given a ticket. He pulled a pizza out of the freezer, stuck it in the oven, and then got a bottle of beer out of the fridge, and tried to relax.

The telephone rang.

Hoping it was Jenny calling from Spokane, he quickly picked up the handset.

"Hello?"

"Ah, Detective," said a deep voice. "I see you finally made it home for the evening."

"What? Who is this?"

"Who do you think it is?" said the voice.

"Is this, AM?"

"Some call me that."

"What do you want?"

"I want *you*."

Even though Wesson was frightened and shaking badly, he tried to go on the offensive.

"What do you mean, you want *me*? Are you some kind of pervert?"

"You shut up! Your days are numbered!"

Wesson's fears began to melt as the caller displayed his anger.

"You're a nothing," said Wesson as he searched for every barb he could throw.

The caller quickly composed himself.

"I have a reason to call you."

"Well, hurry up. I'm getting bored, you piece of slime."

"You won't talk so big after you hear the news."

"What news?"

"You know, Wesson, you should call your wife. She might be worried about you."

The caller then hung up.

Wesson immediately called his wife's parents home and got a busy signal.

Just as he hung up the phone, it rang.

"Hello?"

"George? It's Danny."

"Yeah, Danny. What's going on?"

"We've got another DB."

"Another girl?"

"Not this time. He's nude, his head is gone, and his left hand was chopped off."

Chapter 18
First Direct Contact

Wesson was on the road again, but this time he was going back to the campus. He had another worry. He had tried to call Jenny's parent's home in Spokane, but all he could come up with was a busy signal. He had the operator try to dial the number only again to get a busy signal. Then he called the Spokane Police to have them check the home. That was a half hour ago and he still heard nothing.

He parked his car at the police office and went in. When he entered the lobby, he saw a young pregnant woman talking to Mary, the clerk who was working at the counter.

"I dropped him off at his building the day before yesterday, and I was supposed to pick him up at five o'clock this evening," explained the woman. "He was supposed to go on a field trip to Olympia with his class and spend a couple of nights there, but no one has seen him."

Mary was going through the daily event logs to see if her husband's name would surface. Wesson was taken by the woman's plight and walked to the counter.

"What's going on, Mary?"

"She can't find her husband."

"What's his name?"

"Roger Mills," replied the woman.

"That name's familiar. Where did you drop him off?"

"At the Political Science Building."

"Did you check with anyone inside the building?"

"Yes. I asked other graduate students if they knew where he was, and they said they hadn't seen him at all."

"Oh, here it is," said Mary, as she removed a record from a pile. "Has anyone called you?"

"I don't know. I haven't been home since I dropped him off. I spent some time at a friend's place. Has he been injured? What hospital is he in?"

"He isn't in any hospital. This is an arrest record."

"What? Let me see that!" she said as she snatched the record from Mary's hand.

There was no point for trying to protect her from her husband's lewd behavior and arrest. After reading the report, she dropped it on to the floor. She put a hand to her forehead, and then went out like a light. Lucky for her, and her unborn baby, Wesson was right there to catch her. Someone quickly scooted up a chair and Wesson lowered her into it. After a few minutes, she came to and began to get sick.

"Where is he?" she asked.

"In the county jail, ma'am," replied Mary. "Can someone drive you home?"

"What would I do with my car then?" the woman asked.

"Where do you live?"

"In married student housing."

"That's not far," said Wesson. "Mary, see if there's someone in the break room that can drive her home in her car, and then send one of the patrols to pick him up."

"I'll take care of it," said Mary.

Wesson patted the woman's hand.

"We'll get you home," he said, trying to assure her.

Wesson left her and walked down the hall to his office. His office door was ajar and when he entered, he saw Danny was using his desk poring over some of his notes.

"Hi, George," he greeted him.

"What've we got this time?" asked Wesson.

"We've got another body."

"Where is it now?"

"The county medical examiner has it."

"Any ID on him?"

"Nothin. He was naked."

"How old do you think he was?"

"I dunno. Maybe somewhere between fifty and sixty I'd guess."

"Have you told the chief?"

"I haven't been able to catch him at home."

"Well, you'd better brace yourself when he finds out."

"I took some digital pictures," said Danny. "They're still in the camera."

"Where did you find the body?"

"About the same place as the first one."

"Let's plug the camera into the computer."

In a few minutes, a picture appeared on the screen. It was a naked headless man.

"He wasn't killed here. There's no blood. Probably dumped like the girl."

Danny flipped through several pictures until Wesson said, "Stop."

It was the area of the neck where the head was removed.

"Now, zoom in on the wound."

Danny zoomed in on the area where the body's neck had been cut until the picture filled the computer screen.

"*My God!*" said Wesson. "The head wasn't just chopped off! It was sawn off! Look at the damage. Look at the ragged edge of the wound."

"Man, that musta hurt!" said Danny.

"Has the media gotten hold of this yet?" asked Wesson.

"Sure! They were there taking pictures and interviewing the people. SPD officers were there and were protecting the scene. They're the ones that called us."

"How did they find out?"

"Someone noticed a white van stopped alongside of the road that parallels the perimeter path. He saw a couple of guys getting something out of the van and dumping it in the bushes between the road and the path. After the van left, he went over to see what it was, and then called SPD."

"So when SPD got here, they must have determined it was on the university property," surmised Wesson.

"Exactly."

"How did the media find out?"

"All three TV stations said someone phoned in a tip. Same with the radio stations and newspapers."

"So, that's what he meant when he asked if I had heard the news," said Wesson.

"What? What did you say?" asked Danny. "Do you know who did this?"

Wesson suddenly realized he just exposed Danny to the AM virus.

"Sort of."

"Sort of? Why are you holding out on me, George?"

"Danny, when was the last time you saw the chief?"

"It's been a couple of days. He must be on a trip."

"Without telling anyone?"

"He's the chief. I guess he can do what he wants."

"Let's see if he's home."

Wesson and Danny took patrol car 5 and drove off of the campus. It's been the tradition for the police chief to live in a comfortable house provided by the university. It was about fifteen miles northwest of the campus, located on a hill, in a plush neighborhood overlooking Puget Sound. Because the house was owned by the university, it was legal for campus police officers to enter anytime they felt a need. When Chief Meyer and his family were on vacation away from home, patrol officers were expected to make at least one walk-through a night.

Wesson and Danny entered the circular driveway and stopped in front of the house. Some lights were on, both upstairs and downstairs.

"Looks like he's home," said Danny.

They got out of the car and went up onto the porch. Wesson pushed the doorbell button, but he was not sure it was working. They both banged on the door, and still there was no response.

"Get your weapon out, Danny."

Now with both of them brandishing their guns, Wesson tried the door.

It was locked.

He went to the patrol car and retrieved a set of keys to unlock the door.

Slowly he opened the door a few inches, and immediately they could smell an odor they could only have identified if they had been soldiers in combat, or worked in a slaughterhouse. It was the smell of blood!

"Police officers! Anyone home?" the detective shouted.

Still no response.

The smell was overpowering, and after this night, it would stay with them the rest of their lives.

They decided to search the house starting upstairs and working their way down.

Slowly they ascended the stairs with hearts pounding. When they reached the top, they could see one room with its door open, and a light on inside. It was the same lighted room they saw when they drove up to the house.

Wesson was holding his Glock in front of him with both hands. As he neared the door, he could see it was a bathroom. He kept his gun trained on the doorway as he approached, but he knew there was nothing there to hurt him. He holstered his weapon and stepped into the doorway.

"*Oh, my God*," he said.

Neither man was prepared for such a grizzly sight. Blood was splattered everywhere. There was blood on the walls, the ceiling, in the tub, on the toilet and wash basin. It was everywhere, and the smell of it saturated them.

On the floor were two bodies that were slashed to pieces. They were two naked women. One was likely Chief Meyer's wife and the other his teenaged daughter.

Both officers became sick. They backed up into the hallway and against a wall. Danny vomited, and then they sank to a sitting position on the floor.

"*Oh, Lord! Lord! Lord!*" cried Danny. "How could anyone do something like this?"

"We're not done yet, Danny. We've still got to look downstairs."

"I haven't got the strength to stand up," said Danny.

"Let's just sit tight for a few minutes."

Wesson's cell phone rang.

"Hello."

"George, are you alright?"

It was Jenny. He'd almost forgotten about her.

"Uh, yeah. I'm fine."

"You're scaring the daylights out of us. The police came by and said you called them to check on our welfare."

"I tried to call you and the line was busy."

"The receiver was off the hook was all. Did you think something bad was going to happen to us?"

"Oh, no. Not really. Look, Jenny, I'm kind of busy right now."

"Where are you?"

"I'm on the campus."

"At this hour? What's going on?"

"I can't talk right now," he said and then turned off the phone.

"Come on Danny, let's take a look downstairs."

They raised themselves from the floor and slowly descended the stairs. Neither of them was worried now about being waylaid. They stopped a

Dave Larson

moment in a hallway at the bottom of the staircase before going on. Both men were shaking badly.

"Come on, Danny, we've got to do this."

It was in the kitchen they found the rest of the carnage.

The room was soaked in blood like the bathroom. A serrated knife was on the floor.

They found Chief Meyer's head and left hand lying on the floor.

"We've solved two mysteries tonight," said Wesson.

"Yeah?"

"Yeah. We now know the identity of the DB, and we know why the chief wasn't answering his phone."

"Look on the wall," said Danny.

Written on the wall, in blood, were two letters. AM.

Chapter 19
Back To Business as Usual

Detective Lieutenant George Wesson and Officer Danny Smith returned to their patrol car on legs so weak they could hardly walk. Neither had ever witnessed such a scene of violence and gore. Wesson picked up the radio mike.

"Patrol 5, to radio."

"Go ahead, Patrol 5."

"Call SPD and tell them we have a triple homicide at Chief Meyer's residence."

The desk officer was overwhelmed.

"*What?* The Chief is dead?"

"Affirmative, and the rest of his family. SPD will have to be involved because it's in their jurisdiction."

There was a pause before the desk officer responded.

"10-4."

Wesson and Danny waited for the Seattle Police to arrive. It didn't take long before he could hear the sirens of the approaching cars.

Why are they coming with all of the noise? thought Wesson. *All they're doing is waking up the neighbors.*

The two detectives were standing by their car as the city police rolled up. A man in his fifties got out of the lead car and came over to the two campus officers.

"Who found the bodies?" he demanded.

"We did," said Wesson.

"Who are you?"

"I'm Lieutenant Wesson and this is Officer Smith."

"What is this? Some kinda joke? I've never seen you guys before."

"We're with the University Police."

"You're a lieutenant? You look like you're still in college, kid. I've been on the city force more than twenty years and I'm still only a sergeant."

Wesson's anger was close to the boiling point. He had just witnessed the results of a horrible murder to someone he personally knew, and his family. Now, he's bantering with some guy who's complaining about his job.

"Look, there's a family in there that's been brutally murdered. We haven't touched a thing. Here's my card. We're leaving."

"*What?* You can't leave a crime scene!"

Wesson and Danny got into their patrol car and left.

When they arrived at the University Police office, they were met by everyone who was on the graveyard shift. They all came into the office to hear what they had found. Even the patrols came in to hear the story.

"All I can tell you," said Wesson, they are all dead. It's terrible. Like nothing I could even imagine. It's happened off campus, so SPD is the investigating authority."

"What can we do?" asked an officer.

Wesson thought for a moment.

"You know, we should get all of our commissioned and noncommissioned officers to come in for an information meeting, and let them decide what we should be doing."

"I'll get right on it," said John Hanson, the desk officer.

In about an hour, six sergeants, two shift lieutenants, and the one captain showed up and they all went into a conference room. The time was now three AM. Wesson sat at one end of the table and addressed the assembled commanders.

"Before you hear it from the media, I want to tell you Chief Meyer and his family are dead. Danny and I found them a couple of hours ago. The Chief was beheaded and his wife and daughter were slashed to pieces."

"*What?!*"

"*Oh, no!*"

"*What happened?*"

"*They were murdered.*"

"*Who. . . ?*"

"*How. . .?*"

"By a man who is called, AM. It means Alpha Male. He supposedly is unique in that he may carry an extra 'Y' chromosome making him a super aggressive male and sociopath. What I need to know is what should we do? There are two other people on campus who are also at risk. One is President Denney, and the other is Professor Michael Hunter."

"Why are these people in danger?" asked Captain Gillette.

"It has to do with a news conference held about the murder of a female student. The three main people involved were the Chief, President Denney and Professor Hunter. I think Denney and Hunter need around the clock protection."

"Weren't you assigned to Hunter, by the Chief?" asked Gillette.

"It was to work with him, not to protect him."

"I think your role should change to protect him, 24-7," said the captain.

"What about Denney?" asked Wesson, and suddenly wished he hadn't.

"I'll do it," said Danny eagerly.

"You don't have time to do it, Danny," said Wesson. "Who's going to take care of the rest of our case load?"

"Wait a minute," said Gillette. "Let's figure this out. What we should do is get these guys and their families into safe houses, miles away from here. And keep them there until this thing blows over. Then we can go about our business without spending time with them."

"I don't think we can do it. I think they'll find them," said Wesson.

"Did you say, *'they'*? I thought we were talking about one guy."

"I think there are more than one, or he's figured out how to multiply himself."

"What brings you to that conclusion?" asked the captain.

"Because the murder scenes at the Chief's house were in two different locations, and probably occurred simultaneously. Otherwise one of the victims could have escaped. Then, there was a witness to the dump of the chief's body, and he saw at least two guys."

"All the more reason to remove these targets and hide them they can't be found," said the captain.

"If we do this," said Wesson, "you'd better make sure no more one person knows where they will be located. Otherwise, anyone and families, would be in jeopardy."

"All right," said the captain, "I'll be responsible for getting it In the meantime, I want you, George, to return to your old job. B business as usual."

"I've got a personal request," said Wesson.

"What?"

"I need a couple of days off. I don't think I've slept for 3 days."

"Take as much time as you need, but come back as soon as you can. We've been behind on investigations since you were reassigned."

That was a relief for Wesson to hear. "Thanks."

"But, before you leave, George, I've got one more assignment for you."

"What's that?"

The captain picked up a file from his desk that was labeled, SPD, and removed a fax, then looked up at Wesson.

"Apparently, there is a monthly get-together of faculty members at faculty club. Do you know anything about that?"

"Sure, they give talks about their interests. Professor Hunter gave a talk about sociopaths last time."

The captain studied the fax again, and then turned to Wesson.

"It says here that the next meeting is tonight and SPD will be there to take someone into custody for questioning about the disappearance of his wife, and they want us to be there, too."

"Really, who are they going to arrest?"

Gillette slowly shook his head. "They're going to arrest the speaker; the guy giving the talk."

"No way," said George with disbelief.

"That's what it says here."

"That ought to be quite a show," laughed Wesson.

The captain parceled out more information as he read from the fax.

"It says they'll take him into custody after the meeting and will try to be discrete. They want us there too while they question him."

"I'm tired. I hope I can stay awake through it."

"Well, go on home and get some sleep then come back in this evening. Take Danny with you. He can help you keep awake."

Then, Gillette returned to the subject of AM.

"Is there anyone else this pervert is after?" he asked.

"One other person," said Wesson.

"Who would that be?"

"Me."

Chapter 20
The Problem of Learning

Wesson's alarm went off at four o'clock that afternoon. Still not quite awake, he shut it off and went back to sleep. Later he was awakened again by the phone.

"Yeah?" he answered.

"Hey, George, are you comin' in? It's after six o'clock."

"Oh, Jeez! I overslept. Listen, Danny, you go on over to the faculty club and make contact with the SPD detectives. I'll meet you there."

After hanging up the phone, he quickly cleaned himself up, grabbed a piece of leftover pizza from the fridge and ran out the door. When he got to the club it was seven o'clock and the meeting had just started.

"Good evening," boomed out Professor Anders of the Math Department. "It's nice to see such a large crowd at one of our gatherings. Please feel free to continue eating during the lecture. Go after seconds, or thirds, for that matter."

Wesson saw Danny who was in his civvies sitting on a metal folding chair next to a couple of young men in sport suits. He could spot them a mile away as police detectives. He went over and sat in a vacant chair next to Danny.

Professor Anders pushed his glasses back on his nose and continued his introductory remarks.

"We rotate by department and this month it's the Anthropology Department's turn. Now, whoever is on tap for the lecture takes care of catering the food and drinks. That way we share the duty, and no one gets stuck with the job. Of course we assess ourselves $15 each which takes care of the expenses."

"George," whispered Danny, "they put on a fantastic feed here. Why didn't I know about this before?"

"Shut-up, Danny and listen to the talk. Maybe you'll learn something."

Anders went on.

"That was great food, wasn't it?" said Anders. The stew was to die for. According to tonight's speaker, it was made from a mixture of meats like moose, venison, buffalo, etc. I tell you it was a culinary treat, and I think he should be given a big hand."

The room broke into a shower of applause, whistles and cheers.

"It's time now to introduce our speaker."

Anders again paused long enough to assure he had everyone's attention.

"Our lecturer tonight, I'm sure, needs no introduction to most of us. There are probably only few people today that have earned their doctorates in so many different disciplines. He holds a M.D. and a Ph.D. in psychology and anthropology. Currently, he is the chairman of the Department of Anthropology. Not only did he earn his doctorate in these areas, but he has done extensive studies in math, physics, chemistry and biology. He has done extensive research in many areas of interest and especially on the problems of learning. Currently, he is working on alternate sources of knowledge.

"As an Anthropologist, he has worked on many sites all over the world and studied the histories of ancient civilizations, such as the Mayan.

"I could go on all evening about his expertise and academic accomplishments, but that would be taking away his time with you. So, ladies and gentlemen, I present to you, Professor Harry Chinn."

The room became alive with applause. A bespectacled, tall, thin man of about 45 stood up from one of the front row seats. Anders met him halfway to the podium, where they shook hands and patted each other's back. Professor Chinn walked to the podium with confidence and ease. His facial expressions conveyed kindness, intelligence and power, as he smiled at the audience. Except for his beard, he could have been Harrison Ford, stepping out of one of his "Indiana Jones" movies.

He fussed with the microphone after an attendant clipped it to the lapel of his sport coat.

(Tap, tap) "Is it on? Can everyone hear me OK?"

"Yes," the audience replied.

"How about the recorder? Is it on?"

An attendant nodded.

He organized a few papers he brought to the podium, and then gathered his thoughts as he gazed at the audience.

"I want to thank the University for supporting and promoting our lecture series, and, of course, the faculty club for providing this wonderful facility. I also want to thank you, the faculty, for your attendance.

Chinn paused for a moment as he switched gears.

"Who can tell me some of the methods of how learning and knowledge are acquired?"

A man at one of the tables raised his hand.

"Yes?"

"Conditioned response."

"OK."

Other hands shot up.

"Trial and error."

"Rote," said another.

"Good! You still remember Freshman Psych."

From the audience: "Doctor Chinn, I remember being taught that animals learn by conditioned response, and humans learn by trial and error. Do behavioral scientists still believe that? Has there ever been any evidence that animals too can learn by trial and error?"

"It's interesting that you should bring that up," said Chinn.

"Several years ago, when I was a grad student in anthropology, I went to Africa to help on a dig. We were looking for evidence of the "cradle of humanity". I'd worked for several days in a row and felt I needed some time off.

"I had a small motor bike, and I followed some paths through the jungle just to look around. Then, I saw a beautiful butterfly, like none I've seen before. I laid my bike down and followed it, with hopes I could catch it.

"Suddenly, I stopped and stood still. I could feel something watching me. Then, I saw it! It was a huge male lion. He was fifteen or twenty feet in front of me, partially hidden by the brush. He was crouched, and ready to spring. I knew there is a nerve in a lion's forepaw which runs between the second and third digits. Just before he springs, the nerve will twitch. I kept my eyes on one of his paws and suddenly I saw movement. Immediately, I leapt toward the lion. The lion sailed over my head, and landed exactly where I had been standing. I quickly ran to my bike, as the lion struggled to get on his feet. The bike started with one kick, and I raced away. When I felt I was safe I looked back and saw the lion practicing short leaps."

The audience was stunned. They weren't sure if Professor Chinn had just told a joke or just related one of his many life-threatening experiences. Some of them, especially those who knew the Professor's humor, began to chortle and grin. Most of them, however, just sat there with blank expressions, still thinking about meeting up with a lion that was about to pounce.

Professor Chinn looked down for a moment, then cleared his throat, and went to his lecture.

"So, then I think we can all agree there are different methods of learning, and acquiring knowledge. We all know the learning process for most of us takes many years of formal education, and a lifetime of experiences. Even so, we just don't have enough time to acquire the knowledge needed to be expert in more than one or two fields.

"Unless, of course, we're somehow genetically assembled like Doctor Albert Schweitzer, most of us are destined to be expert in only one or two fields. Doctor Schweitzer had a doctorate in Divinity, Music and Medicine. He was a great humanitarian. He was a missionary to the poor people of Africa, and taught them the scriptures of the Bible. He healed the sick, and when he needed to raise more money, he gave organ concerts throughout Europe and the United States. So, you can see the great benefits high levels of education and knowledge can have on the world.

"What is education, and what is knowledge?"

It was a rhetorical question, but Professor Chinn paused and looked at his audience as though they should be able to answer. After all, these were people who have devoted their live to education. He smiled and then went on.

"Behavioral scientists define education as exposure to something unknown. Knowledge, on the other hand, is the collection of all things we have been exposed to. It is stored as memory, and is available for use whenever the need arises. The pool of memories for each one of us then becomes our basis for "truth" and "reality". It's our total view of the universe.

"But, there are some problems. If the education we receive is flawed, either by errors or intentional lies, then our reality is flawed. What we hold to be "true," is not. This is what Hitler did when he bombarded the citizens of Germany with lies and half-truths. He controlled their beliefs, and they followed him like robots. Likewise, the so-called brainwashing of prisoners of war. Many were convinced they were on the wrong side, and they defected.

"Each time our future generations' senses are overrun by the lies of advertising, political statements, or false portrayals of life from the media, as movies and TV, they are at risk of losing their true views of reality, It is essential we do not let this happen.

"Imagine the damage being done to our kids. There are many single parent families, where the children are left to their own devices, because their mothers or fathers have to hold down a job. They end up watching hours and hours of television. What are they learning? They watch hundreds of hours of murders, thefts, torture, sexual acts, on and on. There is no wonder that they can't learn school subjects through the fog of media "education". We are losing the battle. Each year when we test the school kids we find that their individual pools of scholastic knowledge are becoming shallower and shallower. Clearly, something must be done to salvage the future generations from becoming like "The Simpsons".

"There is some hope on the horizon, for a new kind of "education."

Professor Chinn paused again, to let the statement sink in. The audience was now listening intently. He had just told of a terrible condition, and now he was going to give them a word of hope. He went on.

"Some Behavioral Scientists believe memory exists as a "chemical" within the body. What's interesting here is that it may not just be in the brain, but throughout the entire body. This is not an entirely new idea. In the 1960s, there was a thought that emotions, such as fear, was the result of a secreted chemical.

"Trying to prove this theory has led to an interesting experiment. Researchers put a rat into a small cage rigged with a trapdoor. They hung the cage, with rat, about three feet over a vat of liquid nitrogen. The trapdoor was sprung, and the fall induced fear in the rat, that was quickly frozen by the nitrogen. The hope was by freezing the rat while it was in an emotional state of fear, the chemical could be captured and analyzed. Unfortunately, no mystery chemical was found.

"However, the idea of a "memory chemical" did show some promise. Think of animal behavior. Birds having never been taught how to build a nest are able to do so perfectly the first time. Yet, they still have to learn how to find food, and take flying lessons. All animals, except the human instinctively know how to swim. My colleagues and I believe that there i "chemical", or perhaps are "chemicals" in the bodies of animals that acc for instinctive behavior. We also believe all animals, including humans, somehow manufacture a "memory chemical" for learned behavior.

"Another interesting experiment was done in the 1960s. Researchers took several meal worms, and placed them on an enclosed straight track. The track was walled on the sides, and the only direction the worms could go was either forward or backward. You've got to realize, meal worms are quite small. When I call it a track, think of it as a small track. Something you could put on a desktop, and observe. Some distance down the track was an electric wire that could give a jolt to any of the worms that tried to cross it. As the worms approached the wire, nearly all crossed over it, apparently not knowing what else to do. But, some recoiled and turned back away from the wire. The researchers referred to these worms as "smart worms".

"The "smart worms" were then chopped up and fed to a new batch of worms and they were then placed on the track. When they approached the shocking wire, about half of them stopped and turned back without getting a jolt.

"Now, the experiment ends here. Maybe they ran out of money or meal worms or whatever. So, I tried to replicate the experiment in my lab. Sure enough, about 50% of the second batch turned back, just like the first researchers recorded. But I took things further. I fed the "smart worms" of the second batch to a new group of worms, and about 75% of them became "smart". I kept refining the population, until almost all of the worms stopped at the wire. Oh, sure, there were a few stupid worms in the batch, but not enough to make a difference. This experiment really convinced me a "memory chemical" exists, but I've not yet been able to identify it."

Professor Chinn again searched his audience for reactions. There were none to be seen. Everyone seemed to be on board, and was quietly waiting for him to continue.

"The idea of acquiring memory and skills from unusual sources, or perhaps unusual to us, is not new. The Mayan Indians who lived in Mexico and Central America many centuries ago, is a case in point.

"An ancient city, Chiche'n Itz'a, not to be confused with chicken pizza (ha, ha), was discovered in the Yucatan jungle several years ago. Anthropologists found that these were very advanced people. They built huge pyramid tombs, paved walkways and assembly areas, and aligned arkers to note the seasons. One of the most remarkable things they was to invent a calendar that went on into the future for more than a thousand years. It is amazingly accurate, but mysteriously ends in the year of 2012 of our calendar. Some people believe they were forecasting the end of our world in 2012, but, who knows. Maybe they ran out of materials, or just had no interest to go any farther.

"The thing most striking about the Mayans was their apparent level of intelligence and skill. The large architectural structures they built are so perfectly square, even today's laser alignment measuring tools could not find a flaw. They had a written language of picture words we've learned to read, which has given us a lot of insight about their society. For example, they invented and played a number of games. Some were gambling games, some were board games, but most interesting was a physical game, kind of like basketball.

"The Mayans were great sportsmen, and built huge courts to play their games. The ball court of Chich'n Itz'a is about the size of a football field, and is totally open to the sky.

Archaeologists engaged in its reconstruction found sound transmission became stronger and clearer as they proceeded. A whisper from one end could be heard through the length and breadth of the court. And, the sound waves are unaffected by wind direction or time of day.

"The ball court was the site of a brutal sport. The field was bordered by two imposing walls 26 feet tall. Seven combatants on each team tried to get a rubber ball to go through a small stone hoop 23 feet above the ground, without using their hands. These games predate the Olympics by about 500 years! The games played in the ball court, could last for days, and were sometimes played to the death.

"At the conclusion of the game, the captain of the winning team would be decapitated by the losing captain. You'd think it would be the other way around, but it was a great honor for the winning captain. They believed this act would send the player to a heavenly reward. They then would offer the winner's flesh for consumption to both teams.

From the audience: "Yuck!" "Gross!" "Jeez!"

"Now this was done as a religious rite, and served a purpose. They believed by consuming this guy's body, they would take on his characteristics of bravery and skill. This was only one example of a cannibalistic rite. They had others, such as sacrificing, which gave opportunity for many of them to participate

"Cannibal warriors throughout the unreached tribes of the world, a few generations ago, ate their victims for the same reasons. It wasn' because they were hungry. It was done as a serious religious rite. Probal the Mayan were able to build such wonderful cities, and structures, and had mental concepts to invent complicated games, was because they were able to share from a pool of common memories, which raised the base of their knowledge. There were many Mayan cities throughout Central America, and they all had identical structures and games.

"My staff and I are using cadavers to search for the human memory agents, but so far we've found nothing. In the meantime we are watching our future generations become dumber and dumber. I think if things continue to deteriorate at the current rate, within fifty years we'll be beyond the point of recovery, and our society will simply die out.

"If we could find the "memory chemical" within the human body, it could be synthesized in to a "smart pill". Just think of the good that can come from this. Intelligence quotients could be raised to where we could all become geniuses. Maybe it could become a cure for certain kinds of dementia, and mental illnesses. People who have no purpose, and live on the street, could become useful. The list goes on and on.

"My question to you, then is, what should be done during the time we wait for the "smart pill" to be developed?"

Their eyes became big as they looked at one another.

A Sociology professor, Doctor Cal Schmid, spoke up.

"You're asking *us* what to do?"

"Yes. I'm asking you. What do you think should be done about this horrific problem? I realize you can't dictate policy. That's for the politicians. But, you are educators. What do you believe should be done during the interim. What should be the logical course of action?"

Again everyone's eyes were wide as they sat there without saying a word.

Professor Chinn smiled at them, then said, "It's hard, isn't it? You can't say the word. I'll say it for you. Cannibalism!"

From the audience: What?" "What are you saying?" "Good God, man!" "That's the most absurd...!"

"But, some of you are already practicing cannibalism."

From the audience: "What are you talking about?" "Who's doing that?"

"In a group this size, I'm sure there are a few Catholics here. Each time you partake of the Eucharist, aren't you eating His body and drinking His blood? Aren't you internalizing His attributes? Isn't this why you do this? Also, cadaver parts are used every day throughout the world.

The audience became quiet. Some who were standing now sat down. woman at one of the tables addressed Chinn.

"Surely, Dr. Chinn, there must be some other way."

"If you know another way, let's hear it."

A man asked, "Are you proposing to sacrifice people for this cause? You're not going to chop us up and feed us to our students, are you?"

That comment brought some levity as everyone laughed.

"Hardly. People die every day."

From the floor: "What happens if the one to be... ah, used turns out to be a criminal?"

"There would have to be guidelines to prevent something like that happening."

From the audience: "What if cooking destroys the "memory chemical?"

"To prevent that possibility, the flesh should be eaten raw. It could be mixed in with other meat dishes and no one would ever notice."

From the audience: "What about disease?"

"The flesh should probably be irradiated."

From the audience: "Have you eaten human flesh?"

"Yes."

From the audience: "What was it like?"

"Kind of like pork."

He paused a few seconds as smile crept across his face. Then he went on.

"Which reminds me of the time I got lost while driving through the Midwest. My wife insisted that we stop for directions. We pulled into a farm, and we saw the farmer doing some chores near his pigpen. I walked up to the man, and he graciously helped me. Then he invited me to take a look at his pigs, of which he was very proud. I noticed one pig running around had a peg leg. I asked the farmer,

"What's the story about the one with the peg leg?"

"That one? That's a wonderful pig. He is the smartest pig I've ever seen. And he's so friendly. You know, one night our house caught on fire while we were asleep. That pig broke out of his pen, ran to the house and figured out how to get the door open. He found our bedroom and woke us up. He saved our lives!"

"Wow! But why does he have a peg leg??

"Well, ya know, a pig that good, we just couldn't eat him all at once."

The room erupted in laughter.

"I know you all have a lot of questions, but I'm out of time now, so save them until next time I report our progress, or you can email me.

97

the meantime consider the predicament we're in and what has to be done. Thank you."

The audience applauded and, Professor Anders returned to the podium.

"Thank you professor Chinn. This ends tonight's program, but feel free to hang around and chat. Also, there is still some of that great stew left. So finish it up."

Everyone in the room stood and applauded. This gave Wesson a chance to meet the two SPD detectives.

Chapter 21
Interview

"Hi, I'm George Wesson," he said as he extended his hand to the older of the two SPD detectives.

"I'm sergeant Art Sterns and this is my partner, Ken Gorhoff." Sterns looked to be about thirty years old and Gorhoff in his mid-twenties. Both men looked fit and professional.

Wesson turned around a saw that their quarry was still in conversation with people up near the stage.

Then he turned back to the sergeant.

"How do you want to do this? I don't want a commotion with one of our esteemed professors."

"Well, when he's about ready to leave, we'll step up to him and tell him we'd like a little chat."

Wesson noticed custodians beginning to fold chairs and put them away.

"I'll be right back," he said to the others and walked up to one of the workmen.

"Hi, Sanchez,"

The Mexican smiled.

"Hi, George, what are you doing over here."

"Oh, I just thought I'd get a little education."

"Man, I heard some of that guy's talk," said Sanchez. "That's weird. Imagine eating your way through college"

"Say, is there an office in here I could use for a little while?" asked Wesson.

"The faculty club manager's office is right over there," the custodian said, pointing to a door near the food table and close to where the other detectives were standing.

"That'll be fine," said Wesson.

"I'll unlock it now and when you leave just make sure the door is closed behind you."

Wesson thanked him and then rejoined the other officers.

"Let's take him into that office," he said motioning toward the door, and we can keep everything private."

Gradually, the numbers of people diminished as they left the building, and the kitchen crew picked up what was left of the food and took it away. Professor Chinn finished his conversations with his colleagues and headed for the coatrack.

"Dr. Chinn," Wesson called out as he intercepted him.

"Yes?"

Wesson showed his badge.

"Could we have a word with you?"

"Eh?" responded the professor now surprised as he saw the other three officers approaching.

"I'm Lt. Wesson of the University Police and this is Officer Smith and these two men are Officers Sterns and Gorhoff of the Seattle Police."

"What do you want?" he asked nervously.

"It's about your wife's disappearance," said Sgt. Sterns.

"Oh, you have news?"

"Let's go into this office where we can talk," said Wesson, pointing to the door.

Wesson opened the door and turned on the light. The office was small, but accommodating. There was a desk with an armchair, and four others with straight backs in the room, just the right number for the party.

"Professor Chinn, please take the arm chair behind the desk," said Wesson, while everyone else sat down on the wooden chairs. He deferred to the SPD detectives because he knew nothing about the case.

"Dr. Chinn, could you tell us again when it was that you last saw your wife, Helen?"

"Like I told you, about a week ago," he said with some annoyance.

"What day was that, exactly?"

"Uh, I last saw her on Wednesday. No, it was Tuesday, a week ago today."

"I see. So what was the occasion? What was happening at the time?

"She left on a trip to see her family."

"Was she by herself? Why weren't you with her?"

Wesson noticed the professor becoming pale and more nervous. "Danny, would you find a glass of water?"

"OK, George," he said and left the room.

Then Dr. Chin continued answering the questions from Detective Sterns.

"Well, I was too busy to go with her. I've got classes to teach, grading tests, writing papers…. I don't have time to go off on a trip."

"Do you get along with you wife's relatives?"

The professor looked sad.

"I like them OK, but they don't like me very much."

"Why is that?"

Danny returned with a paper cup of water. The professor thanked him, drank it all and then set it down on the desk.

"They're all academic types," he said. "They are all engineers and business professionals and they don't think my interests are useful or important."

I feel the same way, thought Wesson.

Detective Sterns continued.

"So, you dropped her off at the airport and…."

"*No! No!* I never said I dropped her off anywhere. She took a cab to the airport."

"What time?"

"About eleven PM."

"What cab company?"

"I don't know. She took care of all that."

"What airline? What flight?"

"I don't know! I don't know!" cried the professor frantically.

Detective Sterns now sat quietly for nearly a minute and let the tensions calm down, and then spoke.

"Sir," you know what this is all about, don't you?"

"What do you mean?" asked the professor in a quavering voice.

"You know your wife is dead, now tell us where she is."

"How do you know she's dead?" he asked with tears running down his face.

"We found her blood on the basement floor. It's her type."

Professor Chinn rocked back and forth in his chair, his face buried in his hands which were dripping from streams of tears.

"I didn't kill her. It was an accident. She was leaving and I was trying to stop her. She came up from the basement with her suitcase and I tried to take it away from her. She lost her balance and fell backward down the stairs I could tell she was dead."

"Why didn't you call for help?"

"There was no point. She was already dead. We had been fighting and her family wanted her to leave me. If I reported the accident, they would have said I killed her, and they have a lot of influence."

"So, what did you do with her body?"

"I can't tell you."

"Why not?"

"Because it's too terrible."

"Did you bury it?

"No."

"Did you burn it?"

"No."

"Then what?"

Suddenly Wesson had a thought. "Oh-oh!" he said.

"*What?*" cried Danny.

"The stew! Did you guys eat any of the stew?"

"No." said the two SPD detectives.

"How about you, Danny?"

"No, George! Please don't tell me what you're…."

Before he could finish his sentence, he started vomiting. He got it all over his clothes and the floor.

Everyone in the room was aghast.

Wesson reached over and picked up the empty paper cup from the desk and gave it to Danny.

"Here, Danny. Collect the evidence."

Chapter 22
The Fifty Minute Hour

Wesson opened his eyes and looked at the alarm clock next to his bed.

Wow! Nine AM, he said to himself. *Four hours. That's more sleep than I'd gotten over the past four days.*

He still felt tired, but at least he felt closer to being alive than dead. He knew what he had to do today. It was a secret he kept from everyone other than his wife. He had to make a phone call he dreaded, but he knew it would be much worse for him if he didn't.

Groggily, he made his way to the desk where the phone sat. He opened a drawer where he kept a collection of business cards. Pawing through them, he found what he was looking for.

He laid the card next to the phone, sat down to the desk, and dialed a number.

Ringgg.

"We are assisting other callers," said a recorded voice. "If this is a life threatening emergency, please hang up and dial 911. Otherwise, stay on the line and your call will be answered in the order received." And then music began to play.

Life threatening emergency, thought Wesson. *Yes, it's a life threatening emergency. Only, dialing 911 won't help.*

He sat there listening to the music and rehearsing what was going to say when the live person answered.

Click. "Mental Health," announced a woman's voice.

"What?" said Wesson who was caught dreaming.

"This is the Mental Health Clinic. Can I help you?"

"Uh, I'd like to make an appointment."

"Have you been seen here before?"

"Yes."

"What's your name?"

"George Wesson."

"And, what doctor were you seeing?"

"Doctor Alanson."

The scheduler paused as she searched on her computer screen.

"Can you come in today?"

"Sure. What time."

"Ten AM. Can you get here by then?"

"I think so. How come I'm so lucky?"

"She just had an emergency cancellation."

"I'll be right in."

Wesson first started seeing her during his early years of college when he nearly flunked out. He was smart and knew his stuff, but when it came time to take the tests, he would freeze up. His heart would race, he became sweaty and his mind would refuse to work. The first time it happened, he was afraid he was having heart attack and went to his doctor at the university infirmary.

***

"George, I can't find anything wrong with you," he was told by a physician, "I want to send you to the Psychiatric Clinic for an evaluation."

"*Psychiatry?* Hey I'm not crazy."

"Of course you're not, but there are people who can benefit by psychiatric treatment for a host of reasons."

"I dunno. I sure don't want anyone to know about it."

"Just try it out, George. If it doesn't work, we'll do something else."

Wesson did try it out. First he saw Dr. Hobart, an MD, who spent almost an hour with him.

"Well, George, you have some anxiety problems, and OCD. That's why you're having trouble with the tests."

"What's that in English?"

"It's the kind of person you are. Anxiety is like being afraid. Your heart ·ts faster, your adrenalin starts pumping, you began to sweat and you physically want to defend yourself from a threat, but you can't, because it's the test paper on the desk. Your body is trying to solve the problems physically rather than mentally."

"Wow! I think you're right."

"People with these types of personalities also develop phobias."

"I've heard of phobias but I'm not sure what they are."

"They are unreasonable fears of objects or situations. Do you have anything like that?"

"Maybe. I'm afraid of heights."

"Probably other things too, that you don't realize because you unconsciously avoid them. But, you can't avoid the test."

"You said I also have another problem."

"OCD,"

"What's that?"

"Obsessive Compulsive Disorder, That's a little more difficult to explain. I recommend you have some weekly sessions with one of our psychologists, and then you can explore all of these issues."

***

The treatment he received back then helped him to regain his confidence; to endure the tests and to graduate. He felt free of problems for quite a spell until he got involved with this AM thing. He felt trapped again, and was suffering from periods of paranoia.

Wesson pulled up to the University Hospital parking garage and stopped beside the attendant's booth.

"Hi, George. What brings you down this way?"

Wesson recognized him but couldn't think of his name. All of the parking attendants worked for the Traffic Division, which was a part of the Campus Police.

"I've got a doctor's appointment."

"Man, that was terrible what happened to the chief. Do you have any idea who did it?"

This annoyed Wesson because everyone will be asking the same question.

"Not yet."

"Go ahead and park where ever you want. You don't need a ticket."

"Thanks."

After parking his car, he made his way to the clinic and reported to the reception desk.

"You're right on time, Mr. Wesson. Have a seat and the doctor will come out to get you."

He sat down and picked up a Reader's Digest that was on the table beside him. He began reading an article about the threat of terrorism in America, and then was interrupted.

"Hello, George," said a beaming Annie Alanson standing in the clinic doorway. "Come on back."

"You look bright and cheery today," said Wesson.

"You look pretty good yourself," she responded.

She led him into a room with a large picture window. Wesson walked over to it and marveled at the view of the campus from the fifteenth floor.

"*Wow!* What a view. How much did you have to pay for this?"

"That's what's so great," she said. "It comes with the job."

"Anyone try to jump out?"

"They can't figure out how to open it," she laughed. "Come over here and sit down. You can't avoid me forever."

Wesson sat down in a plush easy chair and Annie on a swivel stool. She was a beautiful woman. She was a couple of years older than he, with blonde hair that came to her shoulders and bright blue eyes. Her voice was soothing and he felt captivated by her charm.

"So, how have you been?" he asked.

"I've been fine, George, but I want to hear about you." She shuffled through her records. "Let's see, the last time I saw you was three years ago. What's happened since then? Are you married?"

"Yeah."

"Oh, too bad," she said with mock disappointment. "Did you finish school?"

"Yes, thanks to you."

"How's that?"

"I think you helped me gain the confidence I needed to keep from going bonkers during a test."

"That's nice to hear. As I remember, you were working part time for the University Police and wanted a full time position after you graduated, did that happen?"

"Yes, and now I have the position of Detective Lieutenant that I've always wanted."

"That's wonderful! So, the reason you're here today is to tell me how happy you are?"

"Not exactly."

"So tell me what's going on."

"I think I'm being stalked by a sociopath and I'm terrified."

Annie was taken aback by Wesson's blunt statement.

"Why do you believe that?"

Wesson, poured out his story, about the criminologist, Dr. Hunter, the prison escape, the dead girl on the trail, the news conference, the harassing phone calls, and finally the murder of the chief and his family.

"And you think you're on this guy's list?"

"Yes."

"George, do you remember when we were talking about your anxiety problem when you would blank out when taking a test?"

"Yes."

"Do you remember some things we learned about anxiety?"

"You told me that 90% of what we worry about never happens."

"Do you think the same could apply here?"

"Doesn't seem like it. I really believe the guy has my number, and he's going to kill me and maybe my wife."

"What makes you think this guy's a sociopath?"

"Because of what Dr. Hunter told me. He believes AM has the XYY chromosomes."

"How did this guy escape from prison?"

"With some outside help."

"And the white van?"

"Probably driven by his helpers."

"Look, George, the reason you're so anxious is because you've made this guy into some kind of monster you can't defeat. He's a human just like you, and probably very smart. However, his weakness is he thinks he can't be defeated.

"You mean, he'll make a mistake."

"Absolutely, and you, George, have the perfect personality to beat him."

"You mean because of my personality flaw?"

"You don't have a flaw, George, you have a *gift*, the perfect gift for your job. What you think of as a weakness may be your strength. Don't defeat yourself by giving him supernatural powers."

"What about my problem with OCD?"

"It would be one of your greatest assets if you want to be a problem solver, or detective."

"Why would someone do something so heinous?"

She seemed hesitant to answer his question, and then looked directly into his eyes.

"I think he's a terrorist."

Wha…?"

"Look, George, you told me he has helpers. A sociopath likes to operate alone. Also, the victims of a sociopath usually have some common trait, like they're all prostitutes, or of a specific age range, and they're all easily accessible. This guy's victims are the one female student and then the police chief and his family. It doesn't add up. And then, the threats."

"A terrorist, though. I thought a terrorist would try to do something big, like a bomb."

"I don't know. Maybe it's to keep you distracted while he's working on something big."

Chapter 23
Danny Smith

Wesson felt much better after his session with Annie. She had opened up avenues he never thought existed and helped to take the power out of AM.

He decided to go to the police office and maybe he could join some of his friends at a table for lunch. When he arrived at the station, he went into the lunchroom and bought a sandwich and a coke from the vending machines. He saw Danny and some of the patrol officers sitting together.

"Can I join you guys?"

"Sure. Sit down," said Danny.

"What's going on?"

"Danny was just telling his stories of when he was on foot patrol," said Officer Jim West.

"Which lie are you telling, Danny?" asked Wesson with a grin.

The patrol officers laughed.

"I'm telling the one about running into the visiting professor behind the infirmary."

"That's a pretty good one," said Wesson.

"OK. Tell us the story, Danny," egged on one of the patrol officers.

"Hey, before I do, I want you guys to see the trick that George can do with handcuffs."

"Danny, I don't want to put on a show," said Wesson.

"Come on, George. These guys have never seen it."

"What's he do?" asked one of the officers.

"You know that Houdini guy?"

"You mean that escape artist about a hundred years ago?" asked another.

"Yeah, that guy," said Danny. Well, George can do the same *thing*."

"Really? Show us, George."

"If I do, how about a hundred bucks from each of you?"

"Aw, come on, George."

"Okay, I'll do it once, but no encores."

He reached into his coat pocket and pulled out a pair of handcuffs and passed them around the table to be examined.

"Regular police issue cuffs, right?"

"Sure."

"I guess so."

Everyone was satisfied.

"Okay, just to prove there's nothing unusual about them, I want someone to try them on."

A volunteer stuck out both arms. Wesson slipped on the cuffs and tightened them.

"Can you get out?" asked Wesson.

The officer struggled and others tried to help him, but to no avail.

"Okay," said Wesson, as he used a key to remove them. "Now, I want someone to cuff my wrists together behind my back."

The volunteer obliged.

"Make sure they're on tight," offered one of the watching officers.

"Now, everyone take a look to see if they're on right," said Wesson.

All were satisfied.

"Now, everyone get up and stand in front of me and no peeking behind my back."

They all stood up and faced him.

"Okay, I want all of you to count to three. Ready? One. Two. Three."

Then Wesson brought his hands in front of him with the cuffs removed from both wrists, and dangling from his right hand.

"*Wow!* How did you do that?"

"That's my secret," smiled Wesson as he stuffed the cuffs back into his coat pocket.

The handcuffs were real, but they had been modified so when they were put on tightly the latching mechanism would release. When he would demonstrate the cuffs by putting them on someone, he was careful not to trip the lock. However, when someone put the cuffs on him, it was natural for them to put them on as tight as possible and thereby unknowingly free his hands. He always carried them in his jacket pocket so he could put on an impromptu show. However, if needed, police issued handcuffs were always available in his car.

Then it was Danny's turn to tell his story, but some were still shaking their heads over the handcuff trick.

"Well, it happened just last June, when we had one of those incredible, beautiful warm evenings. It was about eleven o'clock at night, and a full moon had just risen above the Cascade Mountains. I was walking my beat on the east side of the campus, and I began checking out the student infirmary. As I walked around the building, I stayed in the shadows, so if I come across someone, I should see him before he sees me.

"When I got around to the back of the building, I stopped. About twenty feet in front of me was the silhouette of a man. I watched him for a minute to see what he was doing. Then I realized he was taking off his pants."

"*Really?*" said one in Danny's audience. "Was this guy some kind of pervert? An exhibitionist?"

"Well, that's what I thought, too. So, I walked up behind him, turned on my flashlight, and said, 'Hi!'

"*Whoa!* What did he do?"

"I thought he was going to have a heart attack," said Danny.

"That musta been a shock. So why was he taking his pants off?"

"That's what I wanted to know," said Danny. "So I began to ask questions."

***

"Why did you take your pants off?" asked Danny.

It was a comical sight. Here was a guy, about fifty years of age, standing in front of him, in the middle of the night, without pants.

Wait a minute, thought Danny. *Fifty years old? He's no student.*

The man began to recover from his shock, but was still very nervous.

"I can explain everything, Officer!" he said.

"Can I see some ID?"

"Yes! Yes! Of course you can. I'll get my wallet."

The man picked up his coat that was lying on the ground. He had been well dressed with a nice sport coat, and was even wearing a white shirt and tie.

"Here's my wallet," he said as he dug it out of his coat pocket.

He pulled out some tens and twenties and made sure Danny saw he had a lot of money on him.

"Show me something that has your name and address," said Danny.

"Oh, yes! Yes! Right here."

The man pulled out and handed over a California driver's license, and then a business card that identified him as James R. Kingman, PhD.

"You're from California?"

"Yes! I'm a visiting professor from Berkley, here for the summer."

"Really? Professor of what?"

"Romance Languages."

"Romance Languages? Do you guys usually run around without pants?"

"I can explain."

"Go ahead! I'm waiting."

"Uh...."

It was obvious the guy didn't want to explain and was hiding something.

Danny flashed his light toward the side of the building, and then he saw her.

"What's this?" he said as he moved toward her.

Sitting on a ground floor window ledge of the Student Infirmary Building was a young woman. She had long dark hair that cascaded over her shoulders, and she covered her face with both hands, which didn't help to hide her nakedness. She was convulsing with sobs and shaking badly even though it was a warm night. Danny felt compassion for her and didn't want to cause her more embarrassment.

He squatted down next to her.

"Hi. Can you tell me your name?

"Shannon."

"How old are you, Shannon?"

"Seventeen."

"Are you a student?"

"Yes."

"Where are you staying?"

"In the dorms."

"Do you know this guy?"

"Yes. He's my teacher."

"Did you have a date with him tonight?"

"Sort of."

"What do you mean?"

"He told me he wanted to help me, because I'm so young. He took me out to dinner so we could talk. Then afterwards, we came back to the campus for a walk."

"So he led you back behind the building here. Then what happened?"

"He started kissing me and taking my clothes off."

"Did you tell him to stop?"

"I wanted to. I was afraid to."

"Okay, put your clothes on."

Then Danny went back to the amorous professor who had since put his pants back on.

"What do you have to say for yourself, Romeo?"

"I'm so ashamed."

"Yeah, I'll bet you are. Well, there's no cherry for you tonight, you jerk."

After the girl dressed, Danny gave her one of his cards.

"If this guy bothers you again, just give us a call. I'm going to hold him here for a few minutes while you head back to the dorms."

The girl took the card and left.

"Please give me back my driver's license."

"You can pick it up tomorrow at our office."

"What are you going to do with it?"

"I'm going to use it for making out my report tonight."

"Who will see your report?"

Danny thought for a minute, and then decided to torture him a little.

"They're open records to anyone who wants to see them, and in a case like this, we'll send a copy to your department head at Berkley, and probably one to your wife."

"Please don't do that. What do you want? Money? I'll give you all I have on me."

It was Danny's turn to feel ashamed. He wished he hadn't said anything.

"I'll talk it over with my supervisor. Just come in sometime tomorrow and pick up your license."

The man began to weep.

Danny then left the area and continued on his rounds.

***

" Wow, Danny! That was quite a story," said one of his listeners.

"Ever wish you'd taken the money?" asked another.

"Oh, I've thought about it, but it seemed like such a bad thing to do. I would be just like him. Getting pleasure from someone else's expense. I also wonder how the girl will turn out. I essentially stopped the guy from raping her. I believe God put me at the right place and time."

"Did you ever send a copy of the report to his department or to his wife?" asked Jim West.

"No. The shift lieutenant told me to forget about it. So my report stayed here in the office. He came by the next day and picked up his driver's license."

"He got off without even a slap on the wrist, huh?"

"I know that," said Danny. "How many times has this guy done this in the past? How many more are there like him?"

"You know what I'm thinking?" said Wesson. "I think Danny is one fine cop."

Chapter 24
A New Sales Job

After finishing his lunch, Wesson got up from the table and went to Captain Gillette's office. He tapped on the open door, and the Captain looked up from his desk.

"Hello, George. I thought you were taking the day off."

"I am. I had a doctor's appointment this morning, and on the way back I thought I'd have lunch with some of the guys."

"Can't stand to be alone, huh?"

"Yeah, sure. How are you doing? Must be pretty busy handling the Chief's work as well as your own."

"Oh, I don't know. He wasn't here much of the time, anyway. I don't think he really had much to do. Both Denney and Hunter and their wives are already gone."

"Any news from SPD? Do they have any suspects?"

"Haven't heard a thing. It's gonna be hard to find someone who kills at random and with no reason."

Wesson paused and tried to think how to make his next comment.

"Paul, suppose the killer is *not* a sociopath."

Captain Gillette's eyes grew wide as he looked at Wesson.

"What are you talking about, George? You're the one who's been trying to make the rest of us swallow a story that we're looking for a sociopath. What are you trying to say now?"

"Maybe I was wrong," said Wesson.

"Listen, George. First you come up with a cock and bull story about a sociopath, and you got everyone believing you. Now you say the guy is not a sociopath. What is he then? How did you come to the conclusion in the first place?"

"Michael Hunter originally convinced me the guy was a sociopath."

"What changed your mind?"

"We know there were at least two people involved with the Chief's family murder. A sociopath goes strictly solo."

"Is this something you made up?" said the captain, tersely.

"No. I got this from a reliable source."

"Yeah? Who from?"

"Just trust me."

"Again?"

"Once more. Now, I've got a favor to ask."

The Captain felt let down. He was really angry at Wesson for taking him down the garden path, but he had to credit him for being honest.

"What?"

"I want to meet with Hunter."

"How can you? I don't even know where he is."

"How did you get him into a safe house?"

"I went through SPD. They have contractors for that sort of thing."

"Maybe you could get in touch with them. I've got some more questions to ask him."

Captain Gillette sat quietly for a minute as he thought about it.

"Okay, George. I'll see what I can do. Why don't you go home and get some more sleep? You look awful."

Wesson left the station and headed north on the interstate and arrived home around two PM. He checked his mailbox, but found only advertising fliers, and then he went up to his condo unit.

The reason he and Jenny bought this particular unit was because of the incredible view they had from the fourteenth floor. They had a corner unit allowing them a hundred and eighty degree sweeping view of Puget Sound. They could see the city of Everett to the north, the high rises of Seattle to the south, and all of the smaller communities in between. During the evening hours, they would be treated to beautiful sunsets followed by a light show of traffic on the freeway and arterials. During the daylight hours, although he was seldom around to see it, there would be a parade of ships, both commercial and military, coming into or leaving the harbors. Further to the west, beyond the waters of the sound, were the snowy slopes of the Olympic Mountains. On a sunny day it was a feast for the eyes. Even though there were many days of clouds, rain and limited visibility, it was worth the wait for the sunshine.

He went into the living room, picked up the remote for the TV, and stretched out on the couch. He turned on the History Channel, where WWII was being fought again, and fell asleep.

Ringgg. Ringgg. Ringgg.

Wesson opened his eyes and picked up the phone which was within his reach.

"Hello?"

"George, sorry I woke you."

Wesson yawned and shook the cobwebs out of his head.

"What time is it?"

"five thirty."

"Who is this?"

"Gillette."

"What's going on?"

"We've got another DB."

"Where?"

"Near where the others were found."

"Okay. I'm coming in."

Wesson quickly washed his face, combed his hair, put on his holster and his coat and left.

When he got to the campus, he turned his car on to the perimeter road and continued until he came to an area where several police cars were parked. Men were standing around, looking at something in the ditch.

He stopped and got out of his car. As he quickly walked up to the scene, he spotted Captain Gillette who looked either sad or angry or both.

"Hi Paul, what have we got?"

"Take a look."

Wesson tried to squeeze through the people surrounding the body. They were from SPD, FBI and the Washington State Crime Lab, and of course the media. It was almost dawn but the crime lab people had set up some lamp stands, flooding the scene in bright light. Wesson was close enough now to get a good look at the body. Right away he caught sight of a police nameplate attached to the body's coat.

"*Oh, my God!* He's one of us."

Then he looked at the wounds. Exactly like the chief. His head and left hand had been sawn off.

He looked again at the nameplate, and reality set in.

"*No! Oh no! Oh, God, please, please, no!*"

Then he fell to the ground. There were two medics in the crowd who went to Wesson's aid.

"Hey, Captain. What happened to Wesson?" asked a patrol officer standing nearby.

Gillette turned and looked at the officer, then returned his gaze to the scene in front of him.

"He just learned that it's Danny."

Chapter 25
The Mysterious Stranger

It took a couple of hours for Wesson to control his grief over the loss of Danny. Both he and Captain Gillette sat in the commander's office with the door closed, trying to make sense out of everything that's happened over the past several days.

Gillette was in his swivel chair behind his desk, Wesson sat on a wooden chair facing him. The Captain was deeply affected by the vicious murder of his young officer, Danny. He leaned back in his chair, and fixed his gaze on top of his desk, being careful not to make eye contact with Wesson.

"Why Danny?" he said as his voice broke.

"He must've walked in on something," said Wesson.

"You really don't believe this has anything to do with some 'crazy?'" asked Gillette, now able to look at Wesson.

"Not anymore. From what I've learned about sociopaths, this guy's behavior doesn't fit. A sociopath is strictly a loner. This guy is organized. He has people helping him, and he must be directing them. I think we've all been sold down the river, or conned by a very smart man."

Captain Gillette looked perplexed.

"Why is he killing people?"

Wesson felt like he was beginning to unravel the mystery.

"Maybe he kills to protect his mission."

"What do you think they're doing?"

"I don't know, but it must be something big. I feel as though I'm being watched all the time. I'm sure they're in my condo when I'm not there. I think they even have my phone bugged."

"You still want to see Hunter?"

"Yeah, I was thinking about bouncing the idea of a terrorist off of him, but I'm not sure he's ready to consider that. You know, Paul, I think we're so close to breaking this thing open, and maybe that's why Danny was killed."

"What about the Chief?" asked, Gillette. "Do you think he was on to them."

"I think they killed him and his family to scare us off," said the detective. "Then, Danny stumbled on to something. I still want to see Hunter. He may have some new ideas."

"I'll tell SPD you need to talk with him. Because his location is secret, they'll send someone to take you."

"I might as well stay here tonight. I'm not going back to my condo. I'm positive they've been in my unit, looking for something."

"How can you tell?"

"Everything is in its right place, but not exactly."

"Do you mean you can tell if something's been moved a fraction of an inch?"

"I sort of sense it rather than see it."

Wesson wanted to explain to Captain Gillette that his abilities of observation are heightened because of his Obsessive Compulsive Disorder, but he wasn't sure if he would understand.

"If you're going to be here today, why don't you clean out Danny's locker for me. While you're doing that, I'll get his personnel file. Do you know where his parents live?"

"Somewhere back east."

"Do you want to call them?" asked Gillette.

"I think that's your job."

Lieutenant Wesson got up from his chair and went into the locker room. He opened a maintenance closet door and took out a pair of bolt cutters, which he used to remove the padlock on Danny's locker.

When he opened the locker door, the first thing he noticed was Danny's uniform, fresh from the cleaners, moth proofed and hanging in a plastic bag. Since working with Wesson, he wore civilian clothes. On the locker floor was a pair of rubber boots. A rain poncho hung on the back wall.

Back in the maintenance closet were some empty cardboard boxes. Wesson took a couple and started to fill them. Most of the stuff belonged to the Campus Police, like the uniform, the Glock pistol, and other gear.

Wesson divided the objects from the locker into two boxes. In one were items that belonged to the University Police, in the other were personal items. He looked through them a couple of times, hoping some clue would jump out at him, but there was nothing. He moved the boxes out of the way of foot traffic, and would tell Captain Gillette about them.

He walked out of the locker room and into the front desk area, behind the counter. Mary, the lead office clerk, noticed him.

"Can I help you find something, Lieutenant?"

"Yeah, Mary, where's the daily report log?"

"I've got it over on my desk," she said and handed him a stack of forms.

Each report is the result of a problem or activity that warrants the investigation of a police officer. Wesson took the stack and sat down at a desk, and thumbed his way through the events of the day before.

Just then, a man walked in and stepped up to the counter.

"Can I help you, sir?" asked Mary.

"Yes. I'm here to see Captain Gillette."

"Is he expecting you?"

"Yes, he is."

Mary picked up the phone and dialed an extension. After exchanging a few words she hung up.

"He'll be out in a minute," she said.

Wesson stopped what he was doing and looked at the man.

Must be the guy we're waiting for, he thought. *Nothing looks unusual or special about him.* Gillette came out of his office and went to the front desk.

"Hi," he said. "You're from the security company?"

"Yes."

"Come on back. George, you come back too."

Leaving the files on the table, Wesson got up from his chair and followed the two men down the hall to a conference room. After they entered the room, Gillette closed the door.

"My name's George," said Wesson as he extended his right hand.

The man smiled, and shook his hand.

"My name's Ted," said the agent. "You the one who wants to see Hunter?"

"Yes."

"And, you work for the Captain here?"

"That's right."

"Not anymore. During the time I'm here, you'll be working for me. What's your position, George?"

"Detective Lieutenant."

"Really? You seem kind of young for either a detective or a lieutenant."

That comment didn't go down well with Wesson.

"How do we know you're really a security contractor?"

"You don't. You'll just have to trust me. I don't carry any ID."

Wesson became angry. This mystery man couldn't even show him a piece of ID, and now he acts like he's in charge.

"You're going to have to show *some* kind of proof."

"Listen kid. This is not your show, it's mine. Anyone with half a brain would understand I wouldn't live long if I had to carry proof of who I really am. If you want my help, you'll have to do everything I say, and shut up! Can I make it any plainer?"

The detective could feel his face burning, but took the agent's advice and sat quietly.

"I'll tell you this much. We know we're dealing with a terrorist cell, but we don't know what they're up to. I also want to talk to Hunter to see if we can get some inkling of what these guys are doing. Now, if you're going to give me any static, Lieutenant, you can stay here."

"I'll try to behave" said Wesson between his teeth.

"What's your plan, Ted? How will you guys leave the campus without getting spotted?" asked Captain Gillette.

"Do you know about the campus steam tunnels?"

"Sure," said Wesson. "Every once in a while we walk through them. Sometime we find kids down there and have to kick them out."

"How do they get in?"

"I've always assumed they've found an open door," said Gillette. "There's a large main tunnel from one end of the campus to the other. Smaller tunnels branch off and connect most of the building for utilities, like water, sewage, electricity and steam heat."

"Can I see a map of the campus?" asked Ted.

"There's one on the wall behind you," said Gillette.

"Okay. Where are we located on that map?"

The Captain walked up to the map and pointed to a building near the center.

"We're right here, now."

The agent studied it for a minute.

"Now there's an entrance to the tunnels in this building, right?"

"Yes," responded Wesson.

"Okay, George. Let's say you enter the tunnel here at this building, and you follow it up to that building," Ted tapped his finger on a building at the east edge of the campus. "What building is that?"

Both Wesson and Gillette moved close to see the map where Ted was pointing.

"That's the Central Stores building," said Gillette.

"It looks a little isolated," said Ted.

"It is," said Wesson, "especially at night. You'll never find students in that area."

"Good! That's what we want. George, I want you to use the tunnels and meet me there at nine tonight."

"There? Where's there? That's a big place," said Wesson.

"You find a place to relax and I'll find you," said Ted.

Chapter 26
The Underground Room

Agent Ted left, and Wesson went back to reviewing the Daily Log. Eventually, he found an interesting event. He read the report as follows.

Date: November 25
Complainant: Susan Williams
Location: Old Chemistry Building

Event:
   While walking past the above building, complainant noticed strange odors. Concerned about a possible natural gas leak.

Officer assigned: Daniel Smith.

Wesson discovered Danny worked late that day, and went out on the call about 8:00 PM. No one had seen him since, and it was assumed he had made the investigation, found nothing, and then went on home. He hadn't taken his pistol with him because it sounded like a maintenance problem.

Wesson had about four hours before he was scheduled to meet Ted which would give him enough time to check out Danny's last assignment.

"Mary, I'm going to take patrol car 5 over to the old chemistry building," he said as he removed the ignition key from the key board.

"Okay, I'll sign you out."

"I won't be using the radio, but I'll have my cell phone."

The old chemistry building was replaced by a new building, and was now used for storage. It, and other old buildings, sat on the southern edge of the campus near a stand of trees.

Wesson pulled up behind the building into an empty parking lot. The detective got out of the car and sniffed the air.

The woman reported a strange smell, thought Wesson. *I can't smell.... Wait a minute. I do smell something, but not gas.*

It was just a slight odor. He turned around and in front of him was a staircase that descended underground. It had been so long since he'd been in this area, he had forgotten this underground room.

Years earlier, it was used to store explosives and volatile chemicals. After the Chemistry Department moved their stuff, enterprising students used the room to brew beer. Someone on the campus police force discovered the stash and waited until the brew was ripe, and then raided it. Officers confiscated gallons of the brew and split it up amongst themselves. Since then, the maintenance department put a padlock on the door, keeping out intruders.

At the bottom of the stairs, he reached into his coat pocket and brought out a small, bright, flashlight and directed it onto the padlocked metal door. Looking close at the lock he could see it was foreign because there were no stamped university ID numbers on it. He retrieved a pair of bolt cutters out of the patrol car, and snapped off the lock.

Opening the door slowly, he got a stronger whiff of a chemical odor like chorine. Opening the door wider, he found the room to be pitch-dark. Feeling along the inside wall with his hand, he found a light switch. Now lighted, he could see the room was a jumble of junk left behind by the Chemistry Department.

With his eyes burning from the chemical, he dug out a handkerchief from his pocket and put to his face. The concrete floor was wet from the chemical agent and blood. Following the blood trail to a corner of the room, behind a clutter of boxes and stored sheet metal, he found Danny's head and hand.

He got down on his haunches as he looked at his friend's mutilated remains. Then reaching out his hand, he stroked the hair on Danny's head. He could feel his eyes burning more than ever, mostly from the tears he could no longer hold back.

"I'm sorry, Danny," he said aloud. "I should have protected you. It's my fault!"

He knelt there with his eyes closed, stroking the scull until his thighs could no longer stand it. Then he stood and turned around to examine more of the room.

Danny must have walked into something, he thought. *But, what?*

Having left the door open to the outside, the fresh air began to clear the strong odor. Then he noticed three round vents, equally spaced in the ceiling.

Fans! he thought.

He saw an electrical box on the back wall with a metal handle on the side. He went over to it and pushed the handle up. Electric fans came to life and he could feel the air being changed in the room.

Now he could take his time and began a thorough search of the room. First he looked for the source of the liquid on the floor. It didn't take long before he found a couple of grey cylinders with a nozzle and trigger. He squeezed the trigger on one and a greenish liquid sprayed from the nozzle, with the odor of chlorine. He was sure now its purpose was for disinfecting.

Leaning against a wall were three heavy duty bags. Wesson walked over to them and determined they were of a man made fabric, like nylon. They were very well sealed and whatever was in them looked secure. He lifted one bag and judged it to be about fifty pounds of a powder.

The word "*BIO-TERRORISM*" flashed across his mind.

He suddenly felt vulnerable. He quickly turned off the fans, and the lights, and went out the door. He closed the hasp and attached the broken padlock so at first glance it looked secure.

He got into his car and drove without lights to the south side of the old building. The time was now six o'clock and already dark. He parked close beside the building wall, in the shadows.

Wesson was sure the killers would return soon. They had to finish what they had been doing when interrupted by Danny.

In a situation like this, the procedure is to call for backup. But Wesson reasoned if he called for backup there would be a commotion of officers and cars, and the bad guys would be warned off. Besides, he didn't want backup. He had a score to settle and he didn't want help.

As he waited patiently, he planned his moves. The stairwell down to the room could be used as a trap. He would use the car lights to illuminate the area.

Wesson had never fired his weapon outside of practice, and he wondered how he'd feel about actually shooting someone. Then he thought of all the loss and pain committed by these people. It had to stop.

His thoughts were broken by the headlights of a car turning on to the driveway to the building. The detective's heart began to race as the car's lights were turned off as it continued up the driveway. It stopped at the entrance to the parking lot, and then slowly drove in. The driver turned the vehicle around so he could make a quick escape.

The detective could see it was a van, but in the dark, he couldn't tell the color. It sat there for several minutes. Were they waiting for someone else, or just being cautious? Finally, the doors opened and two figures got out of the van. One of the men went to the rear of the vehicle and opened the double cargo doors. The other man began walking toward the stairs.

This was not what Wesson wanted to have happen. The man going down the stairs will find the broken lock and will know their secret had been compromised. The two men would be separated and difficult for him to deal with.

He took the Glock from its holster and turned on the patrol car's lights. He quickly got out of the car, and moved about twenty feet to his left. Everything became surreal to him. He felt as if he were outside of his body, and watched the scene unfold like a movie.

He began to see everything much more clearly. He now could see the vehicle was a white van. He saw the man behind the van react and pull out a pistol.

"You! Behind the van! Drop your weapon and come forward with your hands in the air!"

The man in the stair well poked his head up, and then quickly ducked down.

The other man stepped out from behind the van and fired a shot, hitting the patrol car.

Wesson fired two return shots into the man's chest. Time nearly stood still as he watched the shooter crumple and fall to the pavement. A crimson pool spread out from the body.

The detective then moved to the stairwell. It was a risky thing to do, but Wesson took out his flashlight and shined down the stairs and saw nothing. He was sure the man ran into the room. He opened the metal door and a bullet ricocheted over his head. Wesson knew if he turned on the lights, he would make himself a target, so he decided to go after the guy in the dark. Both of them stumbled in the blackness playing "Blind Man's Bluff," neither having an advantage.

"Are you the guy that killed my partner?" called out Wesson.

The man fired at his voice, and the detective calculated the shooters position from the gun flash and moved toward it.

"Tell me, do you really expect to have seventy virgins when you die?" Wesson taunted.

Another shot, and another course correction.

"When I catch you, you will find out if the story is true."

"Shuddup!" yelled the terrified man as he fired another shot."

Wesson thought he had him now as he brought up his Glock and emptied its magazine into an area about 20 feet in front of him. He knew he had scored because he could hear the guy scream.

Wesson found the wall and worked his way to the light switch and turned it on.

He found his quarry lying on the floor, sobbing. He was shot in the face just below the right eye. He was a young man, maybe about twenty, and appeared of Middle Eastern descent. Wesson searched his pockets and took out his wallet. Inside he found a student activity card, driver's license, and about $500 cash. Wesson grabbed the man by his hair and lifted him to a standing position.

"Who are you? What is your name?"

He was crying like a baby, almost shrieking.

"I said, what is your name?"

"M-m-m-Mahomid," he stammered.

Wesson drug the man over to Danny's head.

"Who did that?"

"I cannot say! He will kill me!"

"I'll kill you *now* if you don't tell me!"

"Please don't hurt me!"

Wesson raised his Glock and pushed the barrel between the young man's eyes.

"Talk!"

"AM, did it! Please don't let him kill me!"

"You call him, AM?""That's what he told us to call him."

Mahomid was bleeding heavily from the wound in his face. He was weak from blood loss and fell to the floor, crying.

Wesson left the room and climbed the stairs to the parking lot. He pulled out his cell phone and dialed the campus police office and talked to Mary.

"Is Gillette still there?" he asked.

"Yes."

"I need to talk with him."

Gillette came on the line.

"Paul, this is George. Can you meet me?"

"Yeah, where are you?"

"Ask Mary," he replied, not wanting to expose his location over the cell phone.

"Okay. I'll be there in a minute."

While waiting for Captain Gillette, Wesson walked over to the first man he shot and rolled him over. Both bullets hit his heart. He also was about twenty years old and had a student activity card.

He went to his car and got a new clip for the Glock. In a few minutes, Captain Gillette rolled up in another patrol car. He quickly told him what had happened. About the white van that had been seen around the campus and the two men he had shot.

"Let me see the room where the other guy is," said Gillette.

They went down the stairs to where Mahomid was lying in a pool of blood.

Gillette squatted next to the body and looked for a pulse in the neck.

"This guy's dead too."

"I should have called the medics," said Wesson.

"It wouldn't have mattered. He would have died before they got here. Not much you can do with a head wound like that. Facial bones and sinuses are all smashed, and he's got a pretty big exit wound on the back of his neck."

"I got him to talk a little. He said AM did the killing, and they were afraid for their lives. Both these guys had a student activity card, but I wonder if they're fakes."

"Why did they come back tonight?"

"The way it looks to me," said Wesson, "Danny interrupted them loading up the van. They killed him, and put his body in the van then dumped it. Then, either because they were in a hurry or they didn't have room for the last three bags of their load, they came back tonight to finish the job."

"What's in the bags?"

"I don't know," said Wesson, "but whatever it is, they used chlorine to clean up a spill."

The Captain walked over to one and lifted it.

"I think it's about fifty pounds," said Wesson.

Captain Gillette looked worried.

"I'm going to turn this over to the State Police investigation team," said the Captain. "You'd better get a move on if you're going to meet Ted. Uh, wait a minute."

The Captain reached into his pocket and pulled out something and handed it to Wesson.

"What's this?" asked Wesson, as he saw it was an American flag lapel pin.

"It's a locator beacon that can be picked up by satellite."

Chapter 27
The Revealing

Wesson had about thirty minutes to get to the Central Stores Building and meet Ted. He had been instructed to use the steam tunnels to get there, for security. He had a set of keys in his car, which he used to enter the old Chemistry Building, and then the door in the basement leading to the utility tunnels. He found his way to the main north south trunk, and followed it until he came to the intersection for the Central Stores. He then turned 90 degrees to the left and followed a smaller tunnel to the building.

Emerging from the basement, he climbed up a flight of stairs to the first floor. He found an open office, turned on the lights and parked himself behind a desk. He put his feet up and waited. In about a half hour he heard someone open and close the basement door and then ascend the steps. He was sure it was Ted, but just in case, he put his hand on his pistol. He could hear the approaching footsteps, and then Ted filled the frame of the doorway.

"Been waiting long?" he asked.

"About a half an hour," Wesson replied as he put his feet on the floor.

"Before we leave, I want you to hand over your weapon," said Ted.

"*What...!?*"

In a flash, before he could react, Ted's hand went under Wesson's coat and snatched the Glock from its holster.

"What are you doing?" shouted Wesson.

"Shut up! Put your hands behind your back," said Ted, as he now pushed the gun's barrel against the detective's head. He patted him down and found what he was looking for, Wesson's handcuffs. He cuffed Wesson's wrists behind his back then pulled him to his feet.

Ted began to laugh.

"You guys are about the dumbest cops I've seen."

Wesson was silent.

"I just walked up to you and took your gun away," he crowed. "You and your captain," he sneered. "I told you guys a story, and you believed me. That's hilarious."

"Who are you? You really work as a security contractor?" Wesson managed to ask.

"Sometimes I answer their phone," said Ted.

"What do you want with *me?*"

"I've got something special planned, you stupid punk. You're just a kid who wants to play cop."

Ted's cell phone rang.

"Yeah."

"Oh, they were? I wondered what happened. Anyway, it saves us the trouble of getting rid of them."

Then he looked over at Wesson, and said, "Nah, he didn't give me any trouble. These guys aren't cops. They're jokes."

Wesson cringed at the thought of looking inept, but he really was scared.

"What am *I* going to do with him?" Ted continued on the phone. "I've got something really exciting planned. Too bad he won't be able to tell anyone about it. Right. Okay. "

He closed the phone and put it back in his pocket.

"Well, that was a friend of mine," said Ted. "He says someone's killed a couple of our guys. That couldn't have been you, could it? I doubt if you know which end to point a gun. Besides I've noticed you had a full clip."

Wesson now realized it was conspiracy and wondered how many actors were involved.

"Who was that guy? Where is he?"

"Wadda you care?"

"He's that Nazi guy, isn't he?"

Ted laughed.

"I wouldn't even associate myself with someone like that. That just shows how dumb you guys are. Listen, we had someone right under your nose and you never knew it."

"What are you going to do?"

"You'll find out soon enough. C'mon, let's go."

They went out of the building, and Wesson was forced into the back seat of a car and secured with a seatbelt. Then they took a short drive to the University Hospital helicopter pad. A copter was parked away from the center of the pad, leaving room for other arrivals and departures. A pilot was behind the controls and started the engine when he saw them drive up. Ted took Wesson out of the car and put him in the back seat of the aircraft, and then he climbed into the right front seat next to the pilot.

The helicopter immediately took off from the pad. Wesson couldn't tell for sure what direction they were flying, but he assumed it might be east because he couldn't see any part of Puget Sound below him. After about two hours, the pilot remotely turned on runway lights of a small airport below. They landed next to a hangar and got out.

Based on the time they were in the air, and the lack of the lights of civilization, Wesson guessed they were somewhere on the Eastern Washington desert. A cold wind was blowing, and he shivered in the light clothes he was wearing. He looked at the side of the aircraft and saw its origin. A painted logo read, Inland Empire Aviation, Hanford, Washington.

The pilot was still in the cockpit filling out forms, while Ted began looking at something on the left landing gear wheel. He called to the pilot.

"Hey, Tom!"

The pilot looked up from his forms.

"Yeah?"

"Have you seen this wheel?"

He put his forms down on the seat and stepped down to the ground.

"No. What is it?" he said as he walked over to the landing gear.

"You have to get down close to see it."

As Wesson watched, the pilot squatted down on his haunches, Ted pulled out the Glock pistol he had taken from Wesson and shot him in the back of the head. His body pitched forward and rolled over on to its back. The man's blood began to make a crimson lake around his head and shoulders.

Wesson's muscles flinched at the sight, but he made no sound.

"What do you think of that, Georgie?"

"Is that what you've got in store for *me*?"

Ted chuckled.

"Nothing that easy."

"What do you mean?"

"I might as well show you now," said Ted. "You're not going to do anything about it."

He led Wesson to a door in the hangar, and dug in his pocket for a set of keys, then opened it. Inside, he turned on the overhead lights to reveal a twin engine business jet.

"Well, what do you think of her?"

"What am I supposed to think? It's just a plane."

George was trying some psychology on Ted by minimizing everything he would say.

"You think it's just a plane? It's a weapon. A weapon many times more powerful than the planes used on 9/11."

"Come on, Ted," said Wesson, almost jeering him. "What damage could that *fly* do?"

Ted was angry now.

"Look, smart ass. I'm not going to waste this weapon on a building. It's people, not buildings, I want to hit."

"What can you do with a plane like that?" asked Wesson derisively.

"It will be carrying a payload."

"It can't be used to carry a nuclear weapon. They're too heavy. You couldn't get it off the ground. Nope. I don't see you causing any damage."

Ted was frothing at the mouth.

"Of course it's not nuclear! I've never considered nuclear!"

"Oh, I see what's wrong here," said Wesson. "I didn't realize it at first, but this is *your* plan, isn't it. We have a pretty good university here. You probably should have gotten some graduate students to help you out."

"Look, you fool, it's a virus. I know this will work."

At last, Ted began to reveal the plan.

"*Virus?* What virus? What could that be?"

"Influenza," said Ted with a wry smile.

When Wesson first saw the three bags in the underground room, he was afraid of what they might be. By this time, the authorities probably also know what they are, but would have no idea where the rest of it was.

"What's the big deal of influenza? Everybody gets the flu," jibed the detective.

"Not this kind. This is the Spanish Flu virus. It'll kill millions. There's no protection from it."

Ted was so proud of his heinous plan, he enjoyed talking about it.

"So, where did you get it?" asked Wesson trying to learn all he could.

"We mined it from bodies of people who died from it a long time ago and were buried in permafrost. It was mixed with clay, packaged and is now on board the plane."

"What are you doing in this part of the country? How come you're not in a higher population area?"

"You like football?" asked Ted.

"Not very much, especially when we're not winning."

"What day is this?"

"I think it's Friday."

"And the date?"

"What are you getting at?"

"What's the date today?" asked Ted with glee.

"About the 27th…. Oh…. The Apple Cup game!"

"79,000 people!" said Ted. "79,000 people all in one place."

Chapter 28
The Mission

The Apple Cup is the traditional last game of the football season played between the two state universities, the University of Washington in Seattle, and Washington State University from the city of Pullman. Regardless of the teams' standings, you could never be sure who would win. Each year they would switch stadiums to host the cross state rivalry. This year the game was to be played in the University of Washington stadium with 79,000 spectators. It was to be played the next day, and somehow Ted was going to deliver a load of influenza virus. Wesson wondered if it would be a suicide mission, but then doubted it because Ted did not seem the type to give up his life.

"Okay, so you have the plane loaded with virus," said Wesson. "I don't think you're going to fly it into the stadium, and I don't see anyone else around."

Ted gave him a broad smile.

"Let me put it this way," he said. "*You'll* be there when it happens."

Wesson could see he had a big ego and liked to talk about his plan. Maybe he could just get him to expose a chink.

"How did you get involved in this thing? You don't look like a guy on a mission."

"I do this for fun," he said, almost nonchalantly.

"Fun?"

"Yeah, that and money."

"They must pay you a lot," said Wesson, as he kept probing.

"They've got access to a lot of money."

"They must have trained you to do this stuff."

"*They?* Train *me?* You've got it backwards. *I* trained *them,*" Ted said with a snarl.

"Who trained you?" asked Wesson, quickly taking advantage of Ted's flare-up.

"The FBI and the CIA" said Ted, with a maniacal laugh.

"How can you go against your own country? How could you kill that pilot?" implored Wesson.

"It doesn't bother me. I find it enjoyable."

"You're crazy! You are a true sociopath."

"*Sociopath?* I'm not sure what that is. All I can tell you, if someone gets in my way, I get rid of him." Ted said matter-of-factly.

"What about the pilot? What did he do?"

"I just chartered him and I couldn't let him talk about me, now could I? Just like you, George," he said with a grin.

Wesson suddenly switched gears.

"Who is, AM?"

"I don't know, I've never seen him. He ran the show up till yesterday," Ted said with a smirk, "and now, I get to do the grand finale."

This guy fits Professor Hunter's description of a sociopath, thought Wesson. *He has no feelings and he'd kill his helpers when they're not needed. He likes to work alone.*

"Georgie, we've got a big day tomorrow, and I'm kind of tired. So let's turn in. Where's the key for the cuffs?"

"In the same pocket you got the them."

Ted reached into Wesson's coat pocket and found the key. He walked Wesson over to the hangar wall where there was an inch and a half plumbing pipe that ran vertically from the floor to a sprinkler system in the ceiling. Ted took out the Glock, held it his left hand and the key in his right.

"Hold your arms still."

Wesson complied and Ted removed the cuffs, and then re-cuffed him to the pipe. This allowed him to stand or lie down. The concrete hangar floor was cold, but he knew he needed the rest for tomorrow. As he lay there, he began to take stock of everything he had learned and make some guesses of what was probable.

His "ace in the hole" was the handcuffs. He rarely used regular cuffs, because he spent most of his time investigating rather than arresting. Besides, there were other pairs in each of the cars. The handcuffs that Ted had taken from him were not real. They were a prop Wesson used to show off his "Houdini routine," as he did earlier to the guys in the lunchroom. He could escape from them anytime he wanted, but it had to be the right moment or he'd end up dead.

Annie, the psychologist, had told him that the sociopath was not the "sharpest knife in the drawer." He tended to be over confident, and could sometimes make serious errors in his planning. He was a loner and difficult to teach. He is demanding and always wants things to go his way, even at the expense of someone else's feelings, or in some cases, at the expense of someone's life.

Wesson wondered how he could defeat this man. Ted was physically stronger and probably knew how to fight. Wesson couldn't remember the last fight he had been in. It must have been on some playground, many years ago. The other really bad thing was that Wesson was unarmed. Ted had taken his Glock from him and appeared to prefer to use it over his own gun.

He was certain what was in store for him. With no one to fly the business jet, it was obvious Ted would fly it remotely, and Wesson would be along for the ride, killing two birds with one stone.

Gradually sleep overcame him and he couldn't think anymore.

Chapter 29
Flight

The sunlight streamed into the hangar from a window and fell onto Wesson's eyes. He tried to shield them with his hand, but couldn't. Then he awoke and remembered where he was, and that he was in a bit of a spot. On the sidewall of the hangar, he saw an open door to a room where Ted was working on something. Ted saw he was awake and came over to him.

"Good morning, Georgie," he said cheerfully. "It's a beautiful day. A nice day for flying, don't ya think?"

"What time is it?"

"Nine o' clock. Did you sleep well?" he asked mockingly.

"Actually, I did. Thanks for making it possible for me to sleep on the floor."

"Don't mention it. Stand up so I can take the cuffs off."

Ted freed Wesson from the pipe, and then cuffed his wrists behind his back again.

Wesson's mind was racing. He knew if he did anything to upset Ted, he would pay for it. If he showed fear and begged for mercy, it would be pleasing to Ted and inflate his ego. So, he tried to display little emotion.

Ted walked back to the room. "Come over here, George. I want to show you something."

He went to where Ted was standing and looked into the room where he had seen him working. There was an old worn out lounge chair that sat on the floor in front of two large television screens.

"Looks like you're getting ready to watch a football game," said Wesson.

"That's right, I am. But, Georgie, *you* get to go to the game."

"Why do you have two TVs?"

"The Citation uses a map programmed into the auto pilot, just like a cruise missile. There's a TV camera in the nose, and if there's a problem I can override the autopilot with a remote controller and make visual corrections, or I can hit the destruct button and 'bam' the plane gets blown to smithereens. The other screen is for watching the game. I want to watch the reaction of the crowd when the plane crashes on the field, and then explodes, spewing the virus into that crowded stadium."

"So, you think you'll have 79,000 victims?"

"I don't have to. This is my best chance to at least infect a few people. They'll do the rest."

"If it works."

"It's going to work. No doubt about that," said Ted. "And just think. In a couple of hours *you* will see it work for a fraction of a second."

"Why are you picking on *me*?" asked Wesson.

"Because of your news conference. The white haired goat said you were in charge of investigating that girl's murder. So I figured you must be the one to try and find us. You know, we could've killed you several times, but it was more fun to watch you sweat."

"Why do you have to kill *me*?"

"Because that's what I do. It's my job, my business. Besides, you know too much about me."

Ted checked his watch.

"You're gonna have to excuse me, George, while I finish setting things up. You're not gonna get outta those cuffs and we're locked in the hangar, so go find something to amuse yourself with for a couple of hours."

Wesson walked away from the room and looked around the hangar. He didn't know what he was looking for, but he felt it was important to try to memorize all that he saw. He knew he could get out of the cuffs anytime he wanted, but he also knew his move against Ted had to be perfect to succeed. If he made a mistake in timing, he was as good as dead.

The hangar was just big enough to accommodate the Cessna Citation. He went over to the plane and studied it. It looked somewhat abused with a lot of dented skin, and the belly was filthy dirty with dried mud. He tried to imagine what it would be like to be trapped inside, surrounded by one of the most deadly viruses ever known. He knew whatever he did, he could not leave the ground in that plane.

Just behind the pilot's seat was the cabin door and it was open. He saw that it was hinged at the bottom, and when opened, the top of the door folded outward and down to where it almost touched the hangar floor. The inside surface of the door formed steps for passengers and crew. Wesson tried to climb into the plane, but it was next to impossible with his wrists cuffed behind him.

He moved to the front of the plane and saw a television camera mounted inside a small ball turret. *This must be the camera that gives Ted the real time video from the plane*, he thought.

The stress the detective was under became overpowering. He walked to a sidewall and slid down to the concrete floor. He closed his eyes and went to sleep, in spite of the cold floor.

***

"Hey, Georgie Boy. It's time to go. It's the last day of the rest of your life."

Wesson opened his eyes. Actually, he was awake when Ted rousted him. He had been thinking about this very moment. Should he have removed the cuffs before Ted came up on him, and fight him with every inch of his life? He knew he didn't have it in him..

Ted pulled him to his feet and then kept a hold on Wesson's coat collar as they walked to the plane.

"Okay, Georgie, up the stairs with you," said Ted, as he followed keeping his grip.

"All the way to the pilot's seat. Okay, sit down in the seat."

Ted then took the seatbelt and threaded it between Wesson's arms above the cuffs and pinned him to the seat.

"Where did you get this plane?" asked Wesson.

"It came from Central America. It was used for moving drugs."

"Is that why it's so dirty?"

"Probably. They only have dirt strips down there. Well, goodbye George," said Ted who then left the plane and closed the door.

Wesson was already feeling uncomfortable with his wrists being held down by the seatbelt. Within a few minutes, the hangar doors in front of and behind the plane opened. Then he heard a relay switch close and the instrument panel became alive. Soon another relay clicked and the left engine began to start. Seconds later, the right engine began to start. The two jet engines mounted one on each side of the aft fuselage, rose together in a crescendo of noise and power, as the plane shook with anticipation. Then the brakes were released.

Immediately, the plane moved forward out the hangar door. Wesson shed his cuffs, untangled himself from the seat belt, and quickly moved from the seat to the door. By this time, the plane had reached the runway, turned 90 degrees to the left, and was now taxiing to the south end for takeoff to the north.

Wesson saw a red handle above the door and pulled it down. Instantly, he felt a blast of air as the door fell open. He could see the end of the runway approaching and the plane slowed so it could make a 180 degree "U" turn and takeoff. As it began its turn, Wesson rolled down the steps and made a short drop to the concrete. The left wing began to pass over him, and he was suddenly aware that the landing gear wheel was rolling directly toward him. He squirmed, thrashed and rolled and somehow managed to barely get out of its way. He then crawled off the end of the runway and behind an embankment. He was on his stomach and crawled up to where he could peer over the edge of the berm.

The plane started its takeoff run, and Wesson could see the opened door sticking out into the slipstream. As it left the ground and started climbing, it began to drift to the left because of the drag. Then the drifting stopped and the plane stabilized itself in a straight line.

Ted must have taken over manually. I wonder if he knows what happened, Wesson thought.

He made his way back to the hangar as fast as he could. He ran around the building and checked all of the doors to no avail. All windows were about fifteen feet above the ground, but there was nothing to stand on to get to them. He was getting panicky and had to force himself to stop and think.

The building is made of wood, he told himself.

What penetrates wood? he wondered.

He thought of every cutting tool made of metal, but could find none.

He tried again.

What destroys wood?

The first thought that came to his mind was fire.

He looked at the helicopter with its dead pilot lying next to it.

He walked over to the machine and examined it. He found a fuel cap and opened it. He took a sniff. It smelled like kerosene. Then he remembered last night when it was starting up. It sounded like a jet engine. It was a turbine. The fuel's not as flammable as gasoline, but still it burns.

Looking more, he found a fuel drain at the bottom of the tank. Inside the copter he found a few quart sized paper cups marked for air sickness. He filled one cup with fuel and set it down on the ground. He couldn't find any matches but there was a cigarette lighter on the instrument panel. He took some of the forms the pilot had been working on just before Ted killed him, and dipped them in the fuel. He pushed in the cigarette lighter and when it popped out it was red hot. He touched a corner of the paper to the lighter element and softly blew on it. Suddenly, a small flame flared and ignited the page of paper. He stuffed the burning paper into another paper cup, picked up the one with fuel, and quickly took them to a sidewall of the hangar.

He splashed about half of the fuel on the side of the building, and then ignited it with the burning paper. Wesson watched the fire and added more fuel until the cup was empty. He stood back and let the fire do its work as it grew in to a small inferno that reached the roof. There was no interior wall and soon Wesson could see inside where the fire had broken through. He took off his coat, wrapped it around his forearms and held it to his face as he pushed his way into the hangar through the wall. He picked up a two foot long scrap of lumber from the floor. Frantically, he ran to the room where Ted was struggling to keep the plane in the air. The door was closed and locked. It was a cheap hollow core interior door used for privacy more than security. He tried to break it down by running into it with his shoulder and managed to crack the thin plywood panel. He tried kicking and managed put a hole in the panel about the size of his fist. He inserted the end of the two-by-four board between the two panels of the door and pried them apart, pulling the latch open.

"You're too late, Georgie!" Ted called out, as he sat in his chair and steered the plane, already on final approach to the open end of the stadium.

Chapter 30
Attempted Assault

As soon as the Citation left the hangar, Ted had closed the big doors and was now sitting in his chair, watching the scene through the TV lens in the nose of the plane. He could hardly believe what he was seeing. The plane had just taken off, and was starting to go off course.

"What's going on?" he cried.

He got up from his chair and turned on the manual flight controller that was a panel on the bench in front of the computer monitor. Immediately, speed, heading, and altitude appeared beneath the video images from the nose camera. Connected to the computer was a joy stick which allowed him to take manual control of the plane.

As he struggled to keep the Citation flying on a constant heading, he turned the turret that housed the camera so he could look at the bottom part of the plane for damage.

"*Oh, no!*" he cried, as he saw the open door hanging from the left side of the fuselage.

"How could he do that?"

Now he knew Wesson wasn't on the plane, and he was sure he was going to see him again soon. He couldn't leave the controls to look for him without the loss of the mission.

Ted was furious he didn't kill Wesson while he had the chance. He thought it was a great idea to put Wesson in the plane to ride along. It would make a statement of being invincible if they found the detective's body in the wreckage.

He experimented with different power settings and found that the airspeed of 300 miles per hour had the least amount of buffeting. It was going to take about fifty minutes to reach the stadium, and he had to manually fly it all of the way.

When he had thirty minutes left, he could hear Wesson outside of the hangar rattling doors to find one open. Both his gun and Wesson's were in the pockets of his jacket lying on a chair about fifteen feet away. He didn't think the plane could stay aloft for the few seconds he'd have to leave the controls to retrieve them.

Even though he was overriding the autopilot, the terrain following system was working. It was set for 200 feet above the ground, and it maintained altitude to prevent the plane popping up on radar screens. If it reached an altitude of 500 feet or more in controlled airspace without a flight plan, bells and whistles would go off in FAA and Department of Defense radar sites, and the plane would have a lifespan measured in minutes.

When the Cessna began to climb over the Cascade Mountain Range, about fifty miles to the east of Seattle, he only had to keep it on a straight course as the terrain following system took care of the altitude requirements. As it flew through Stevens Pass, many heads were turned, and some cars ran off of the road because of the sight of a low flying jet with a door hanging open.

When the plane crossed the summit, the terrain following system automatically brought it down at the same rate as the downward slope of the western side of the range. Suddenly, Ted realized the plane was lined up on an outcrop of rock, but before he could react, the plane's internal terrain avoidance system automatically added power to the engines and the nose rose, allowing the plane to easily climb over it and then automatically return the control back to Ted.

Soon the plane was over the east shore of Lake Washington and directly across the water, Ted could see the objective, the horseshoe shaped Husky Stadium. From this perspective, the end view of the north and south covered stands, looked like gaping jaws. Between the "jaws" is the open end of the horseshoe, the entrance for the plane.

He made minor adjustments to the heading and power and began the final approach to the stadium. He now manually overrode the terrain avoidance system on his handheld controller so he could crash the plane on to the football field.

Ted could smell smoke and knew Wesson had set fire to the hangar. Then he heard pounding on the door to his room, and then crunching sounds as the door was being dismantled by Wesson. When the door opened a cloud of smoke came into the room with Wesson. The plane was now passing only a few feet above the masts of yachts, moored at the stadium docks by football ticket holders. Ted knew Wesson was behind him, but he was so close to the completion of his mission, he couldn't take his eyes off the screen.

"You're too late, Georgie!" he called out.

Chapter 31
The Apple Cup Game

The last football game of every season is the Apple Cup. Two cross state rival teams, the Washington State Cougars and the University of Washington Huskies alternately play the game in their home stadiums. This year the televised game was being played at Husky Stadium with the action described by sports announcers.

Bob: "We have a timeout here at Husky Stadium with five minutes left in the first half of the Apple Cup, and the Washington State Cougars are leading the Huskies 14 to 10. We'll be right back after these messages."

While the broadcasting stations were taking their break, Bill Jennings swept his binoculars to the east and on to Lake Washington. At first he thought he saw a bird off in the distance, but it was getting larger.

"Bob, train your binoculars over the lake. Is that a *plane?*"
"Where?"
"Look straight out, about twenty degrees above the horizon."
"Oh, yeah. It looks like a biz-jet. What's he doing?"
"It almost looks like he's lined up for a landing on the field."
"Look at the monitor. They've got a good view of him, and look, the cabin door is open. I think he's going to crash right on the *field*!"

The announcers were signaled they were back on the air.

Bob: "We're back again at Husky Stadium, and we have an event taking place. On your screen you can see a business jet that appears to be trying to make an emergency landing on the football field. The officials on the field have now noticed the plane and they're clearing the area."

Bill: "The fans in the closed end of the stadium have noticed the plane now and there's a mass exodus taking place.

Bob: "He's just entering the stadium! He's too high to land. I think he just went to full power, and the nose is pulled up in a steep climb. Here he *comes*! *Wow*! He just missed the stands! He's making a climbing turn to the left, back over the lake.

"Folks, I want to tell ya, when the plane came by he was at eye level with me. I had my binoculars trained on the cockpit, and there was no one in there! The cockpit was *empty*!"

Bill: "There's total pandemonium here. Thousands of fans have fled the stadium including many of the *players*! I don't think anyone wants to play football after what has just happened. We've been scanning the skies with our binoculars and can't see any sign of the plane now. "Folks, this is the strangest day of my *life*!"

The drag of the open door, on the left side, caused the plane to turn to the left. The air pressure from the increase in speed broke the door hinges, allowing it to separate from the plane and fall into Lake Washington. The plane continued climbing up to 40,000 feet and turned to a westerly direction. The FAA and Homeland Security people suddenly became aware of an attempted terrorist attack, and went into action. Two F-18 fighters were scrambled from nearby McChord Air Force Base and were directed to find and destroy the Cessna Citation. Two hundred miles west of the Washington coast, it suddenly disappeared from FAA radar scopes. The fighter pilots reported all they could see was a glistening sheen of oil on the surface of the water.

Chapter 32
Rescue

After breaking through the door, Wesson didn't hesitate. He brought the two-by-four board back over his right shoulder and swung with all his might, as if it were a bat. The board struck Ted along the right side of his head. He fell out of his chair in a spray of blood and lay on the floor. The flight control joy stick had fallen from his hand and on to the floor, striking the disconnect button and returning control to the autopilot in the plane. The plane was now being controlled by a scuttle program that had been installed by some drug cartel to get rid of incriminating evidence, namely the plane and its cargo, and was sending it west over the Pacific Ocean.

Wesson hit Ted one more time to make sure he wouldn't get up. The smoke was getting thick. He saw Ted's coat on a chair and grabbed it in case it had some evidence in it. It felt heavy. He checked the pockets and found his Glock pistol. As he turned around, the smoke had gotten so thick he became disoriented. The hangar was blazing. A bolt of panic went through him. He had to get out quickly before he died from the smoke.

"Georgie! Where are you? Help me out," Ted called out.

I guess I didn't hit him hard enough, thought Wesson. He didn't answer him. He found his way out of the room and was now in the main hangar where the fire was. In fact, the fire was all over; in the ceiling, the walls, everywhere. He moved to be in the middle of the hangar floor and he stood there. There was no fuel for the fire in that place and the air seemed better, but he knew it couldn't last long.

"*Please,* George, help me! Please! Please!" Ted's voice was pleading and nearly screaming.

Still Wesson didn't answer him. He didn't want him near. He couldn't trust him. The pleading went on for what seemed a long time. Eventually, it stopped.

Things weren't looking well for Wesson either. He couldn't decide what to do, and it was getting hotter. The smoke was swirling around him, now. He knew he didn't have much time. He lay down on the floor for air and found the concrete cool to his face.

This might not be such a bad way to go, he thought.

He began to hallucinate. He thought he heard something like a motor. *Maybe if the smoke could be seen by a town somewhere,* he thought, *they'd send out a fire truck. Probably wouldn't get here in time.*

Suddenly, he heard a different noise. Some banging sounds, and then someone calling.

"*George,* where are you?"

"*Over here!*" he managed to call back.

Then he saw a figure coming through the smoke. It was Captain Gillette. And there were others. They grabbed him by the arms and pulled him outside. Nothing looked better than the sunshine and blue sky.

Captain Gillette and two members of the State Police had been brought in by a National Guard helicopter.

"You guys couldn't have timed this any closer," said Wesson.

"It was the locater lapel pin that led us here."

"Oh, yeah. I forgot about that."

"Well you must still have it. We picked up the signal on a GPS tracker. I don't see it on you, though. Is it in your pocket?

"No."

"Where is it," asked Gillette.

"When I was waiting for Ted at Central Stores it occurred to me if anything bad happened to me, how could I be found? I never did trust Ted and I was afraid he might take it from me, so I swallowed it."

Chapter 33
Closure

"Michael! Welcome back," said Detective Lieutenant George Wesson as he stepped into the professor's office.

"Believe me. It's good to be back. I heard you had quite an adventure."

"You might say that."

"Do you think Denney and I were really in danger?" asked Hunter.

"Probably not, but at the time we felt it was better to be safe than sorry," said Wesson.

"I thought surely AM was after me. He sounded so angry when I didn't give him credit for the study," said Hunter.

"Maybe he was, but I don't think he was going to risk the mission just to get at you."

"What about Chief Meyer? Why was he and his family killed?"

"Nobody knows. Maybe it was just an act of terrorism, like the girl. They were causing a big diversion to protect the mission. But, I was on their list too, because *you* guys set me up with the news conference," said Wesson as he narrowed his eyes at his mentor

"I'm really sorry we did that," said Hunter.

The detective relaxed his countenance and smiled again.

"I've got a little surprise for you," he said as he handed the professor an envelope.

"What's this?" he asked as he opened it.

"It's from Dr. William Barnes. He says the XYY chromosomes were present in the specimen sent to him."

"What specimen? I didn't send him anything," said the professor.

"I did."

"Well, what's this about?" said Hunter with a puzzled look.

"I had a sociopath's blood on my pants. I cut out a piece and sent it to Dr. Barnes. He confirms it has the *'superman'* chromosomes, and I'll confirm by observation that he was a sociopath. So your theory still holds together," said the detective.

"What about AM? He should have the XYY," said the professor, as he leaned back in his chair.

Wesson sat down in a chair facing the professor. Still smiling, he looked at Hunter a moment.

"That's right, Michael. It wasn't AM who was in the hangar with me. His name was Ted, and he's the sociopath whose blood I sent to Dr. Barnes. But, how did you know there were two guys."

Hunter looked confused.

"What do you mean, George?"

"Well, I told you I had a sociopath's blood on me, and you seemed to know it was not AM's. So you must know there were two men."

"You've lost me, George. I can't remember what I said now," said Hunter as he began to nervously drum his fingers on his desk.

"AM wasn't a sociopath. In fact, he was a very highly organized terrorist who hired a sociopath."

"Well, George, thanks to you it's finally over," said the professor. "I don't think they'll try it again."

"There are still a few problems to worry about," said Wesson matter-of-factly.

"Such as?"

"We still don't have any idea where AM is, and I don't think his superiors are too happy about him failing his mission. It must have cost them a lot of money and time. So you see, Michael, this case isn't solved, yet."

"Well, it's as good as solved, isn't it? I mean, you were able to stop the attack on the stadium, and these guys will never come back. Obviously, the man who held you prisoner is dead."

"We never found his body."

"Maybe, he was consumed by the fire," the professor suggested.

"You mean, without a trace? I don't think so. No, he got away and, by now, he's probably already back here somewhere."

"To do what?" said, Hunter. "You think they'll set up another attack somewhere?"

Wesson notice a line of perspiration beads beginning to show on the professor's forehead.

"The way I see it, Michael, he's probably planning a scheme to save himself by shifting the blame on to someone else."

"To someone *else*?" parroted the professor.

"Yeah! When the girl was killed, you and I were the only ones actively investigating. I think someone was telling him everything I was doing so he could keep ahead of us."

The color began to drain from Hunters face.

"Look, George, it was probably someone in your own department. Maybe he was discovered by the chief and that's why he was killed."

Hunter was becoming frantic, now.

"No, the girl and the chief were killed to keep everyone busy while the virus bombs were being built at the old chemistry building. Danny was killed because he walked into their operation."

"You don't think *I* had anything to do with it, do you?" cried Hunter, now nearly in a panic.

Wesson now knew the truth. Hunter gave himself away through his panic. He admired the man so much that he could barely stand the thought of his mentor as his betrayer.

Then, softly he asked, "Michael, how did AM escape the prison?"

"I-I don't know. I was unconscious at the time. He must have had help from one of the staff members."

"You helped him, didn't you?"

"N-no! Look what he did to my hand!" cried Hunter."

"I've thought about that. It occurs to me you were given a choice. You could lose your hand, or you could lose your life. You chose to lose your hand, but you also lost your soul. To him! From then on he owned you. You would do anything he asked."

Distraught, Michael Hunter slumped in his chair. He was quiet for a moment, and then said, "What are you going to do, George?"

"Well, I have no proof. No one will ever believe me. So, I'm not going to do anything. I won't tell a soul."

A spark of life came back to Hunter. He sat up a little.

"You'd do that for me, George? You won't make any accusations?"

"That's right."

"You'd just let this go away?"

"Yep. Only...."

"Only, what?"

"Well, there're a couple of bad actors out there somewhere, and I don't think they'll want to take the blame for the failure. Also, I don't think they'll want anyone talking about them either."

"Oh," said Hunter as the realization hit him. "But, *you're* going to protect me, aren't you?"

"From what? This is all speculation. The University Police is finished with the case. It's a Homeland Security thing now."

Wesson's cell phone rang.

"Wesson here. When? I'll be right there."

He closed the phone and then looked at Hunter, still slouched in his chair.

"I've got to go, Michael, Someone just robbed a cashier at the HUB."

And then he left.